WILL GALLOWS AND THE ROCK DEMON'S BLOOD

Derek Keilty

Illustrated by Jonny Duddle

First published in Great Britain in 2013
by Andersen Press Limited
This Large Print edition published 2013
by AudioGO Ltd
by arrangement with
Andersen Press Limited

ISBN: 978 1471 343698

British Library Cataloguing in Publication Data available

Printed and bound in Great Britain by
MPG Books Group Limited

To my wife, Elaine,
with love

Chapter One

★

Magic in the Stable

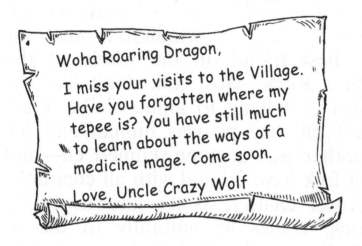

Woha Roaring Dragon,

I miss your visits to the Village.
Have you forgotten where my
tepee is? You have still much
to learn about the ways of a
medicine mage. Come soon.

Love, Uncle Crazy Wolf

Folding the letter, I tucked it into my shirt pocket, then, heaving a sigh, I entered the stable.

'Where are we going, Will?' my horse Moonshine asked eagerly as I walked into her stall on Phoenix Heights, our ranch.

'We're going nowhere, Shy,' I replied, patting her on the nose which,

1

like the rest of her, was pale as a wraith. 'Except to brand those new calves out by Silver Brook.'

Moonshine is a mute-winged windhorse and my best friend on the whole of the West Rock. Most folk don't like the idea of talking to animals. But I am half elf—my pa was human and my mother was a green-skinned elf—and elf folk have a bond with all creatures. Critter chatter, as it's known on the rock, comes as naturally to me as herding cattle. But today even Shy couldn't cheer me up.

'Wow, your face is even longer than mine. What's wrong, Will?'

'Got another letter from Uncle Crazy Wolf asking when I'm gonna visit Gung-Choux Village.'

'Great! When are we going?' she

nudged me with her nose.

'That's just it, we're not. Grandma says there's still way too much work to be done on the ranch.' Yenene, my grandma, was stubborn as a mine pony, and there was no arguing to be had with her. 'It's so frustrating, Shy,' I went on. 'Grandma wants me to go brand calves when what I really want to do is visit my uncle and get practising my elf magic.'

'Can't you practise here?'

'With all the extra chores of the ranch I got no time. And I want to learn *new* stuff not just keep going over the same few things I can recall.'

Phoenix Heights was our third ranch. The first, Phoenix Creek, had been destroyed when part of the Great West Rock collapsed due to years of illegal mining. Yenene and I, and many others, lost our homes when the whole of the western arm broke off the rest of the rock and fell into the Wastelands below (the West Rock had at one time resembled an enormous cactus but now it didn't look like anything much). Our second ranch, Phoenix Rise, was over on the eastern arm, but we'd sold it when we moved up here to the mid-rock four months ago. We'd sold it cos Yenene said it was too small. At the time Moonshine had joked, 'Phoenix Creek, Phoenix Rise, Phoenix Heights—pretty soon we're gonna run outta Phoenixes!'

Moonshine's saddle was sitting on the rack. Opening a pouch in it I found a small container of elf face paint. I sighed again as I looked at it. Some brave I'd turned out to be. Before we moved I'd been initiated into the Gung-Choux tribe—my great-uncle's tribe. I was even given an elf-brave name—Roaring Dragon. But it seemed like no sooner had I become part of the tribe than I'd abandoned them, along with my studies of elf medicine magic. And elf magic was something you needed to keep practising to perfect.

'Looks like Roaring Dragon won't be doing much roaring. I won't be needing face paint for quite a while—maybe never.'

But I couldn't resist. I smeared a thin red and yellow stripe—the colours of

4

an elf brave—on my cheeks.

'What about those magic books I used to see you reading, couldn't you learn new stuff from them?' Shy tried to encourage me.

'Yeah, if I could find them. But I haven't seen those books for weeks now. I'm pretty sure Grandma has hidden them cos she doesn't want me learning elf magic. In fact, I'm certain she moved us all the way up here just so I wouldn't be as close to Gung-Choux Village and Uncle Crazy Wolf.'

'Remind me again why she hates it so much?'

I sighed. 'She says elf magic has a dangerous, dark side—but she ain't told me any more than that. There's definitely something she's keeping to herself.'

Even though Yenene felt so strongly about magic, the stable walls were decorated with old elf artefacts: a drum, a decorative peace pipe and a painted rock-buffalo skull that when I was little made the hairs on my neck stand up. My pa used to take it down and chase after me, scaring me with it, until we'd both collapse on the barn floor laughing. Pa had been a deputy sheriff till he was treacherously murdered by his own boss, the former crooked sheriff of Oretown. It still made me real angry just thinking about it.

Next to the old artefacts hung my bow and a quiver full of arrows. I took them down. 'I was getting so good at arrow bending too.'

I raised my bow, aiming the arrow to miss the pillar in the middle of the stable. The idea was to use elf magic to focus on the arrow as it flew, and, with the power of magic, bend it in midair to hit the target (useful if your enemy or prey moved very quickly). But I was far too rusty and the arrow shot straighter than a rifle barrel, disappearing into a dark corner at the back of the stable.

Moonshine shot me a hopeful grin. 'It was close.'

I sighed. 'It was miles away.'

'Try again,' Moonshine urged, trotting over to remove another arrow from the quiver with her teeth.

'It's no use, Shy. I've forgotten it all.'

'Try again,' Moonshine mumbled through the arrow shaft, and I chuckled taking it from her teeth.

Then I heard a strange noise coming from the back of the stable, something like snapping twigs, coupled with a low growling sound. A louder spitting noise followed and pieces of arrow shaft were suddenly catapulted through the air, landing on the ground near my feet. I froze, feeling my heart gallop inside my chest.

'Who's there?' I called into the darkness.

'*Mmmmmmmrrrrrrgggggaaabbula!*'

Moonshine gave a nervous snort and backed up. 'Sounds like a whip-tail goblin sneak thief.'

I wasn't sure. 'Don't think so, not unless he's got a bad case of indigestion. No, I've heard that growling sound before.' My mind raced back to a time I'd stood in a dark creepy cave in the heart of the underground city of Deadrock. A chill ran down my spine as suddenly I had a pretty good idea what the intruder might be.

'I think it's a wraith!'

Moonshine's ears shot up. 'Did you just say *a wraith*?'

I nodded, feeling my heart race like a steam train on full throttle.

'Like the wraiths that live in Deadrock?'

'Yup they—'

Before I could say another word, the huge apparition of a horned beast with long pointy fangs and clawed hands and feet glowed in front of me, shimmering like a ghost. A wraith is a ghost-like, undead creature that haunts desolate places. And this one was even more terrifying than the wraith I'd seen before! The collapse of the western arm had released a lot of them from their rocky homes, shaking them out like lice from a sky-cowboy's pants.

'It *is* a wraith; big one too.'

Moonshine gasped. 'Oh, great! Now just tell me why it had to come into *my* stable—there are loads o' stables round here!'

My legs felt wobblier than one of my grandma's chokecherry jellies. My instinct was to mount Moonshine, ride through the door and fly off, but the wraith would most likely follow us outside, maybe even attack the other ranch hands or Grandma.

For the moment the wraith was just assessing us from its dark corner.

'We gotta think fast, Shy. Wraiths can suck out your soul and leave you like the walking dead!'

Moonshine shivered. 'OK, way too

much information. What are we gonna do?'

I spotted Grandma's Wynchester Demon Shot rifle—the only weapon capable of snuffing out a ghost or wraith—on the stable wall and dropped my bow. But I couldn't reach it, and even if I could, the wraith was in the way. Deciding it had nothing to fear from a boy and his horse, the thing moved slowly out of the gloom.

'I need that demon shot, Shy!' I hissed.

'How in the world we gonna get it?'

'Well, there is something I could try to buy us some time. You can bind wraiths and demons, sort of freeze them. Uncle Crazy Wolf taught me.'

'Do it!' she cried.

The wraith fixed me with a ghostly glare.

I grabbed the rope from Moonshine's saddle and began looping it into a lasso. A normal lasso would just pass clean through the spirit, but with the right spell this rope could take on magical properties. I just had to get it right.

The wraith moved closer, growling now.

'I can't remember the spell properly. Spirits alive, I can't remember it!'

'Great,' said Moonshine. 'If we get out of here I'm gonna give Yenene a piece of my mind for hiding those elf-magic books. C'mon, Will, you can remember, you can do it!'

My mind was blank with fear but I had to overcome that. The spell! The spell! I knew for sure you didn't need dried herbs or anything like that, the way you did with healing or conjuring magic. All you needed was concentration and the right magic words. Problem was I couldn't remember the right magic words.

With supernatural strength, the wraith picked up a wooden barrel and flung it at me. I only just managed to duck out of the way as it crashed into the stable wall. Shrieking with frustration, the wraith then lifted a pitch fork and came towards me with even more venom, brandishing it back and forth, forcing me to stagger backwards.

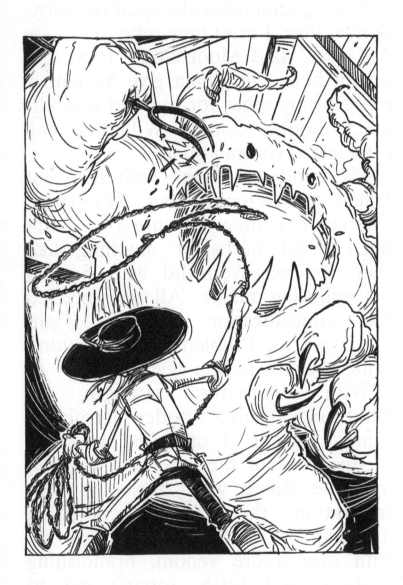

My wise uncle's painted face flashed in my mind as I finished tying the knot and began swirling the lasso above my head. I had to do this, I couldn't let him down.

At last the magic words sprang into my head.

'Hwan wakipa yakan klos kaga!'

Nothing happened. I must have missed something.

'Maaahaaahaaahaaaaaarrmmgula!' The wraith roared, with a sort of twisted laughter, as it thrust the pitch fork towards me.

'Do something, Will!' whinnied Moonshine, moving to stand at my side.

Beads of sweat began to run down my cheeks. *Focus. Have to focus.* I tried the spell again, only this time changing the magic words a little.

'Hwan yakan wakipa hakin kaga!'

Suddenly the lasso began to glow with a pale blue, ghostly light as I twirled it above my head. My heart gave a leap. I'd done it! But, no, something wasn't quite right. The glow should've been a steady, almost

13

blinding, light but instead it flickered weakly, at times almost fading out.

'It . . . it's not powerful enough, Shy. I can't do it!'

Hissing and spitting the wraith swung back the pitch fork, obviously hoping to put more holes in me than Grandma's salt shaker.

'You *can* do it!' she cried. 'Just focus.'

She was right. I took a deep breath and focused again. The spell I'd managed was weak but maybe, just maybe, it was enough. The wraith's gurgling noises grew louder; its eyes widened, blinking like a marsh toad. I tossed the rope. My aim was true, and with a deafeningly loud hiss—like plunging a red-hot branding iron into a pail of water—the loop fell around the wraith's glowing horns. At least I'd got the non-magic part right. Next, I pulled the loop tight, repeating the spell.

'Hwan yakan wakipa hakin kaga!'

The creature gave a loud roar, dropping the pitch fork. The faint blue light from the rope now shot down its shimmering body as it stood frozen to

14

the spot, arm still aloft, eyes staring.

'You did it!' cried Moonshine. 'Is it dead . . . undead? You know what I mean.'

'It's bound by the magic, kinda like spiritual handcuffs and leg irons. But not for long—the magic's weak, thanks to my lack of practice.'

Even as I spoke the light was already beginning to fade and I saw the wraith flexing its great clawed hands, growling, ready to come at me again.

'I can't let go of the rope, Shy, and I need that demon shot—quick!'

Moonshine sprang into action and, hurtling across the stable, she snatched the Wynchester Demon Shot from the stable wall using her mouth. Then, with a flick of her strong neck, she sent it flying through the air towards me. Moonshine's aim was equal to my roping skills and I caught the gun by the barrel end.

I would never forget the time I'd been dangerously close to a vicious wraith before—in a Deadrock tin mine. It had emerged from the mine wall and I'd seen it attack some troll

15

miners, sucking out the souls of the few who couldn't run quick enough. That was till one fella showed up with a Wynchester Demon Shot!

Now it was my turn. Not letting go of the rope for a second, I took aim. I was pretty sure I detected a look of fear flash across the wraith's face as I squeezed the trigger, and, with a roar, a blinding beam of white light surged from the two skull-shaped barrel ends. The bolt of energy tore into the evil spirit. Yelling demonically the wraith began to diminish; its ghostly outer form dropping off to reveal a phantom skeleton of pale glowing bones. Then they too began to melt away into nothingness. The wraith was no more.

'*Yeeehaaaaaa!*' Moonshine hollered. 'We showed him who's boss.'

'Critter won't be bothering us anymore, that's for sure.' I lowered the rifle. A few puffs of smoke spewed out of the barrels and twisted up into the stable.

Moonshine looked admiringly at it. Sure was an awesome weapon. The demon shot had been invented years ago by an elf gunsmith—it had magic tucked away inside its cold steel.

'See, I knew you'd remember the spell.'

'I got lucky with the magic, Shy, I'm so outta practice. If it hadn't been for you tossing me that demon shot . . .'

'My pa always said, "There ain't no 'I' in TEAM". We did it together, Will. Like always.'

I placed the rifle carefully back on the stable wall then lifted down a saddle from the rack. 'I'm kinda shook up but there's chores to be done—you OK if we make a start out for Silver Brook to brand those calves?'

'Sure thing, though don't be expecting my legs to carry us too straight for a little while, my knees are still knocking.'

I started saddling Moonshine for the ride to Silver Brook when Grandma poked her head round the stable door.

'You OK, Will? Did I hear some shootin' as I was on my way over?'

'I'm fine, Grandma.' I wondered whether to tell her what had happened, she was always worryin' 'bout me. But

17

in front of her stern look I couldn't lie. 'I had a visit from an angry wraith. Don't worry, I got it with the Wynchester.' Though she didn't seem to have a problem with the magic hidden away in the rifle, I deliberately didn't tell Yenene about the binding spell I'd cast. Part of me wanted to let her know that instead of being dangerous, elf magic had just saved my life and most likely hers too. But what was the point? There was obviously something she wasn't telling me and I needed to figure that out first.

Grandma shuffled inside the stables, pulling her black shawl tight round her shoulders—the day was misty and gloomy. Long elf ears protruded from the silky grey hair that hung down to her waist.

She tutted, gawking at me. 'See you been smearing that stuff on your face.'

I put a hand to my cheek. I'd forgotten about that. 'I found some elf paint Uncle Crazy Wolf gave—'

'Hope y' ain't been practising magic. I've told you before, elf magic is dangerous and you shouldn't be meddling with it. That brother of mine should know better. I just wish he'd listened to me when I tried to talk him outta becoming an elf mage.'

'It's not dangerous, Grandma, not if you use it right. You just need to keep practising, and that's something I haven't been doing—I've forgotten most of it.'

I couldn't convince her. 'Can't say I'd be worried if you forgot *all* of it.'

'Why is it you're so against me learning elf magic? You go on about it being dangerous, but being a sky cowboy's just as dangerous if you don't have the right teaching. Uncle Crazy Wolf's a brilliant teacher. He wouldn't let me come to harm, you know that. You're not usually one for worrying about a bit of danger so there must be more to it. But you've never told me. What is it?'

'Your uncle don't understand the real dangers of the dark side.'

'And you do? Even when I was little you told me I couldn't do elf magic on account of me only being *half* elf. Why, Grandma?'

'That's enough questions, Will. I've said my piece, and while you're living under my roof I want you to quit practising that magic.' She breathed a sigh. 'Anyway, what I came here to tell you is that you got a visitor.'

'A visitor?' I was intrigued. 'Who?'

'The sky cavalry!'

Chapter Two

★

The Scorpion Pendant

Bewildered, I followed Yenene inside. What could the sky cavalry want with me?

I was gobsmacked to see my friend Jez standing in a brand-new sky-cavalry uniform, her usually tousled mop of black hair tucked neatly into a cap. The sky cavalry is an army of brave soldiers under the command of the High Sheriff, the ruler of the West Rock.

'Spirits alive, Jez, you're . . . you're a soldier!' I gasped.

'Sure am. No more stirrin' pots o' cook's beans—give you more wind than a rock tornado—in the fort kitchen for this dwarf,' she beamed.

Jez is a prairie dwarf and sharper than the little bone-handled knife she always carries. We became good friends a while back when she helped me track down Pa's murderer. Since then she'd been working in the kitchen of Fort Mordecai, the cavalry base overlooking Mid-Rock City, not too far from our ranch.

'I'm blown away. That's amazing. When'd all this happen? Ain't that long since I last saw ya.'

'Only last week. The captain came striding into the kitchen one afternoon saying the High Sheriff wanted to see me and I'm thinking, *Oh no, what have I done wrong? Maybe he's gonna complain about lunch or something.* No way did I expect him to offer me a job as a trainee soldier. Basic training lasts for a few months and then if you do OK you pass out and you're a *real* soldier.'

I was tickled pink for my friend. 'You'll do fine, Jez. Reckon you'll be a real asset to the sky cavalry. You're quick thinking, clear minded and the bravest dwarf ever.'

She blushed. 'I love the uniform too,' she said brushing her jacket down. 'Ain't ever felt so smart.'

'And I guess they're OK with you wearing your pendant?'

She put a hand to the oval pendant around her neck—a scorpion encased in smooth amber on a leather thong. 'It's a pity, but they ain't actually, it must've slipped out on the journey over. Remind me to tuck it in 'fore I go. I hate not wearing it in case someone takes it or I lose it. I wouldn't part with it for the world.'

Yenene gave me the pendant when I was little but I'd given it to Jez in Deadrock for saving my life in the deep mines.

'You oughta think about becoming a soldier too, Will—you'd be great. And as for a horse, well, I know for a fact you wouldn't have to ask Moonshine twice if she wanted to join the sky cavalry.' She laughed, and I followed her gaze outside the window to where Moonshine was deep in conversation with Jez's cavalry horse.

'He'll do no such thing,' Yenene piped up from where she was tidying the kitchen. 'He's a sky cowboy not a soldier. I got plenty for him to be doing around here.'

Jez grinned, she and Yenene had

always gotten on. She went on, 'At the minute I'm mostly doing stable and guard duties but the High Sheriff says I'm doing so well he's got a special job for me. Tomorrow I'm riding with a detachment of soldiers to Deadrock to join the excavation team. I guess you've heard about the tunnel landslide that's trapped everyone inside.'

I shuddered. 'Yeah, I think it's terrible . . . But you're kidding me, right—you're not really going down there?'

Deadrock is a dark underground city deep inside the belly of the Great West Rock, lit only by the eerie purple light given off by branches of the magical saddlewood tree. It's a favourite hangout for goblin gunfighters and snake-bellied troll outlaws.

'No, I'm serious. Cos I used to work in the tin mine air vents down there, they got a mission for me to crawl along them, the way I used to, and get a message to the mayor that we're still trying to get everybody out. I'll be

taking some vital medical supplies with me for the sick folks too.'

I remembered the time, a while ago, when I'd rescued Jez after she'd got trapped in one of the vents. I was quite surprised she seemed so cool about going back down there—and that the cavalry were giving her such a big job when she was still only training.

'Sounds kinda dangerous what with all the rock subsidence since the collapse of the western arm.'

'I know, but I'm well used to it with the bad rock quakes when I worked there. They're saying I'm the only one who could do this. Now, ain't that something?'

'Just be careful, Jez. Ain't them has to go in there, it's you.' It sounded dangerous; there were lots of stories of late about trolls looting and starting fires over on that part of the rock. But although I was worried for her, I couldn't help feeling a tiny bit jealous; it was bound to be more exciting than ranch chores here, especially when I wasn't even allowed to practise my elf magic.

'I don't *have* to do it, and I know Deadrock's full of outlaws, but there are good folks live there too, and somebody's gotta help them. I lived in the place long enough so I should know. The High Sheriff's anxious to try and free Deadrock before troll anger boils over into conflict.'

As we talked I was suddenly aware that Grandma kept hovering close to Jez, staring at her, then frowning and mumbling to herself. She was acting kinda weird and I felt embarrassed. What was she doing? She normally loved it when Jez came by.

Jez seemed to notice too, and kept moving out of the way, perhaps thinking Grandma was looking for something beyond her.

I decided not to make a deal out of it and asked Jez, 'Can't the Mid-Rock City trolls help the sky cavalry? It is mostly their own people they'd be helping to free.'

'The cavalry won't let them, in fact they've banned the trolls from the site of the excavation.'

'Why?'

Mid-Rock City Times

BURIED ALIVE!
MID-ROCK CITY TROLLS
DEMAND MORE
OF HIGH SHERIFF
IN FREEING
DEADROCK FOLK

'Some went to help after it first happened but they just made things worse. They went in axes blazin' almost causing another landslide.'

She pulled out a copy of the *Mid-Rock City Times* from her bag and tossed it down in front of us. Her finger drummed the page. 'Some snake-bellied troll is real mad with the High Sheriff and at the way things are. He's set himself up as a voice for the trolls, and he's been organising big protest rallies at the gates of Fort Mordecai

28

every night. Ugly critter—goes by the name of Jake Sixsnakes—'

Suddenly Yenene dropped the plate she'd been carrying over to the sideboard.

Jez stopped. 'Ma'am. You all right, ma'am?'

I put my hand on Grandma's arm. Snake-bellied trolls are the evilest kind of troll you could meet with; real snakes pouring out of their guts, horrible little oily black heads and flickering tongues. But it wasn't like Yenene to be so shook up at just hearing about one.

Tutting, Yenene stooped to pick up the broken pieces. 'I . . . I'm fine, old fingers that's all.'

'I'll do that,' said Jez stooping to help.

As she did, Yenene made a grab for the dangling scorpion pendant Jez wore, catching it in her palm, staring fixatedly at it.

Jez's face took on a look of bewilderment. 'Ma'am? You OK?'

Yenene let the pendant slip through her fingers. 'Quit fussing, will you?'

29

I'd been worrying of late that she'd maybe bitten off more than she could chew with the new bigger ranch. She was usually so composed and it was kinda weird to see her acting like this.

'I-I'm fine. It's just kinda stuffy in here.'

But she didn't look fine. Her face had drained of blood. She took the newspaper Jez had brought and shuffled outside. 'I think I'll get some air for a bit.'

I followed her onto the stoop, leaving Jez inside. 'What's wrong, Grandma?'

She peered over the paper. 'Nothin'.'

'Ain't nothin'. Tell me.'

'I'm tired, and . . .' She sighed. 'Well, OK then if you must know it upsets me seeing Jez wearing the scorpion pendant I gave you.'

'But I gave it to her ages ago.'

'First I knew of it. Anyway, that's not the point.'

'I didn't just give it away for nothing. I gave it to Jez cos she helped me track down Pa's killer.'

'But of all things to give away.'

'I wanted to give her something nice to show her my appreciation, and the pendant was mine to give. Why are you getting so worked up about all this now?'

'Cos that pendant belonged to my mother and it should remain in the family.'

I was starting to feel a bit guilty. I had no idea the pendant had meant so much to her. But I couldn't ask for it back, wouldn't be right. 'She doesn't know you gave me it,' I admitted.

'Keep your voice down,' Yenene said then coughed and wheezed till I thought she was going to have a heart attack. I felt torn—on one hand I could understand why Grandma might be upset on account of the pendant being her mother's, but on the other hand I could still remember how Jez's face had lit up the day I'd given it to her.

'Look, if it makes you feel better maybe I could try and think of some way of asking for it back. I don't know how, but I'll try.'

Yenene nodded. 'I can't think the sky cavalry would encourage her having

31

it, anyway, on account of it not bein'
part of the uniform. Whoever heard of
a soldier wearing a pendant?'

I fetched her some water; she took
it from me without saying anything, so
I headed back inside and noticed Jez
over by the window, fastening her bag.

'I gotta go,' she said stiffly, not
looking up.

'Go?' Now both of them were
acting strange. 'But you just got here.
I thought you'd wanna see Shy—I'm
taking a ride over to Silver Brook to
brand the new calves, you want to
come?'

'Thanks, but I can't. I told the High
Sheriff I'd only be a couple of hours.
I'm riding for Deadrock tunnel at dawn
so I gotta get plenty of rest.'

I spotted the pendant on the table
and my heart sank into my sky-cowboy

boots. I grabbed it and held it out to her. 'Jez, look, wait! You weren't meant to hear that. Pay no mind to Grandma, this is yours and I want you to have it.'

'S'OK, Will. I'm glad I heard. You shoulda told me it was an heirloom. It's fine, really. She's right, y'know, something like this should be kept in your family.'

She made for the door, and, still holding the pendant, I followed.

'Jez. C'mon. Take it.'

'No. I can't. Look it ain't like I'm gonna fall out with ya over it.'

But she didn't look too happy with me right now. 'I'll make you another. One you can keep. I'll make you one, Jez. I promise I will.'

'Don't worry about it; you got your hands full working a big ranch here. I'm gonna be too busy to miss it, and least I won't have to worry 'bout losing or damaging it now.'

'I'll have it for you when you next visit.'

Jez's voice sounded strange. 'Probably not be riding by for a while on account of my training and this mission to Deadrock. So don't go to any bother.'

'How long you reckon you'll be in Deadrock?'

'Dunno. Maybe a few days. That's if a big fat dust rat don't jump out and get me, they're full o' surprises . . .' She shot me a testy glance. 'Kinda like people, I guess. I really gotta go. So long, Will.'

I followed her outside where she mounted her mare then rode off without so much as a wave. My heart sank. Jez had seemed pretty upset, I was worried we might not be friends anymore.

I walked back to the end of the porch where Grandma rocked on her rocking chair apparently engrossed in reading the paper. I was pretty sure she'd been listening in to Jez and me, though.

'Hope you're happy now, Jez has gone. She left this.' I opened my palm, the amber casing of the pendant reflected in light. 'She heard us talking.'

'She'll get over it. Heard you say you'd make her another one. You could have it for next time she visits.'

'That's if she ever does. I gotta feeling she won't be back for quite a while, she looked upset when she left, and I can't say I blame her.'

I went to leave. Those calves wouldn't brand themselves. But Grandma's eyes were fixed on the pendant. She grabbed my wrist. Her grip was tight and it took me by surprise. She spoke firmly, 'Put it on, Will.'

Still a bit stunned by her behaviour, I slipped it over my neck.

'I want you to promise me that you'll never take it off. It's more important now than ever. Do you hear me?'

'Is something wrong, Grandma?'

She didn't answer. 'Promise me.'

'OK, OK, I promise.'

'Good.' She rocked for a bit, humming to herself then said, 'Well, what are you standing there for? Get over to Silver Brook. And wipe that stuff off yer face—no call for a rancher to be wearing brave paint!'

★   ★   ★

I hardly said a word to Moonshine on the ride to Silver Brook. I was deep in thought about how strange Grandma was acting. I s'pose I could understand why she'd get upset about me not paying enough mind to the pendant being her mother's, but what about her reaction when Jez had mentioned the troll called Jake Sixsnakes? Now I thought back on it, it was even stranger, almost as though she knew him.

I thought about Jez too, and my stomach churned remembering her trying to sneak off, leaving the pendant on the table. Jez loved that pendant—it bugged me the way everything had happened.

And there were bigger things on my mind. I envied Jez for knowing what she wanted to do with her life. She'd often said how she'd love to join the sky cavalry, and now she'd got her dream job. I was older than her yet still didn't really know for sure what I wanted to do. Oh, sometimes I thought I did. Ranching was OK, and I was pretty good at it, but it wasn't my whole drive and passion the way it was Grandma's. Right now I yearned for the tepees and towering totems of Gung-Choux Village and I longed to learn about medicine magic. I decided that whatever Grandma thought, I was going to learn.

Chapter Three

★

Rustlers

The next morning it was grey again, which fitted my mood perfectly. Branding the calves had taken my mind off stuff, but it had all come rushing back soon as I returned to the ranch.

Not being able to sleep I decided I had time before breakfast to search for Uncle Crazy Wolf's magic books. As I crept down the stairs I tried to think of places Grandma could have hidden them. I searched under the couch and armchairs in the living room—even lifting up the cushion on Grandma's rocking chair, but no sign. Next, I checked the kitchen drawers and cupboards. Still nothing. What had she done with them? I knew they must be somewhere. Unless she'd gone the whole hog and thrown them away . . . I paused for a breather and backed up, straight into Grandma's pot stand— pans clattered noisily over the kitchen floor.

'Great job, Will, just wake up the whole o' mid-rock,' I breathed. I stayed still as a dead gutfish hoping Grandma wouldn't catch me, and after a few moments everything was quiet again.

Out in the hall, I realised I'd forgotten about the plank gun cabinet. Heart beating, I moved over to it, but save for Grandma's rifle it was empty.

Then I heard some floorboards creak upstairs.

'Will, is that you?' Yenene called from the landing.

'Yeah, just me, Grandma.'

'Rock quake wouldn't make half as much noise—what in spirit's name are you doing banging about down there?'

'Couldn't sleep, so I figured I might as well get on. I'll make a start on breakfast, you getting up?'

'I s'pose I will, I'm awake now, thanks to you.'

★   ★   ★

Grandma seemed to be back to her old self while we ate breakfast, though

40

I was still thinking about my books and not really concentrating. I did see her clock a glance at my neck to check I was wearing the pendant, but she made no comment about it. She had just started writing me out a note for supplies she needed from the city when Tyrone, our head rancher, came bursting into the kitchen, breathless, his face drained of colour.

Grandma stared at him. 'Tyrone, what is it?'

'Got us some trouble, ma'am. Big trouble. Rustlers have stolen a head of about thirty calves over by Silver Brook.'

'Silver Brook,' I gasped. 'But I was out by there only yesterday, branding those young 'uns.'

'They drove 'em away right from under our noses. I'm back to round up all hands. We're going after them!'

'I'll come with you.' The elf-magic books flew straight out of my mind.

'No,' Yenene snapped. 'It's too dangerous, Will. Could be snake-bellies. It's gloomy enough for them to be out and about.'

'Can't follow the rustlers. Can't visit Uncle Crazy Wolf! Can't learn magic! What can I do, Grandma?' I blurted angrily.

She looked taken aback. I was too. I hadn't really meant to raise my voice so much. Tyrone dropped his eyes awkwardly.

I cleared my throat, then softening my tone, I went on, 'Besides, won't be the first snake-belly I've had to deal with.'

'That's what I'm afraid of.'

Still looking at the floor Tyrone coaxed, 'Sure could use all the men I can get.'

'I'm not a kid anymore, Grandma, I can look after myself.'

She sighed. 'You better go, then. Just be careful, the whole lot of you. And take some of my broth with you— keep you going.'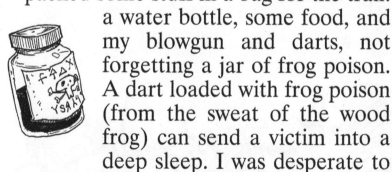

Tyrone was in a hurry to get off so I gave Grandma a hug and quickly packed some stuff in a bag for the trail: a water bottle, some food, and my blowgun and darts, not forgetting a jar of frog poison. A dart loaded with frog poison (from the sweat of the wood frog) can send a victim into a deep sleep. I was desperate to put one into a cattle-stealing troll.

Out in the stable I called, 'We're out o' here, Shy! We got us some rustlers to catch up to.'

'Rustlers?!' Moonshine whinnied

loudly as I saddled her up. 'Why, I got two rock-hard back hooves just itchin' to make a permanent imprint on their good-for-nothin' behinds.'

Rusty, one of the ranch hands, hobbled over as we prepared to leave. He'd broken his leg a few weeks ago, falling from a ladder while fixing the roof. 'Wish I could ride with yez an' help y'all catch 'em.'

'You rest that leg, Rusty,' Tyrone called. 'We need you back in the saddle for the cattle drive next month.'

Lifting his hat, Rusty thrust it in the sky. 'I will, hang one o' the low bellies high for me.'

★　　★　　★

We rode a dusty trail out of Phoenix Heights, it was too misty to fly and, besides, we had to keep on the ground to pick up the trail of the rustlers. Tyrone and all of the ranch hands had riled expressions on their faces. There's nothing more hated on the rock than a rustler, my pa used to say.

'Something funny 'bout the rustlers taking our calves,' Ty commented as we rode.

'What do you mean?' I asked.

'Well most rustlers like unbranded calves, that way they can sell 'em on easily. Can't understand why they didn't take 'em before yesterday when you shoved a red-hot branding iron on

their little butts.'

It was strange. 'You're right, Ty. Sounds like they're either stupid or maybe they just don't care.'

Steering in close to me, Tyrone muttered, 'Will, I want you to have this for protection.' He reached over and handed me a gun belt with a six-shot blaster in the holster. 'I was gonna give it to you before we rode out but I didn't want your grandma making a fuss.'

Hands trembling a little, I took it from him, fastening it round my waist. 'Yeah. OK, thanks, Tyrone.' It suddenly hit me these rustlers would be armed too and might not be ready to give up their stolen steers without a gunfight. I was just glad to have Moonshine with me—she was good in a fight and the best horse a sky cowboy could have.

'Don't be shootin' anyone now.' Ty grinned. 'I mean you to use it to scare 'em off.'

I smiled. 'I'll try not to.'

We rode to Silver Brook where the now-stolen calves had been grazing: a wide-open grass prairie, featureless save for an occasional gnarled saddlewood tree. Then Ty led us off again.

'We'll be lookin' for a set o' hoof prints, will we?' I asked the old rancher.

'S'right, Will,' he nodded approvingly. ''N' these rustlers don't seem too fussed 'bout hiding themselves, so I don't reckon it'll take us too long to find 'em.'

He was right. We soon discovered that the rustlers had driven the calves north, in the direction of the Edge Mountains. As I looked closer I saw that the hoof prints of the rustlers' horses were different to Moonshine's, heavier, more like the print of flightless animals. Troll horses!

'Reckon it's snake-bellies or rattlethroats we're after.' Tyrone said what I'd been thinking.

'There's been more problems with trolls lately, hasn't there? You think maybe it could be the same group that's been blamed for starting all them fires they been reporting in the papers?'

'I heard about that and about lootings too in some of the smaller villages out in the country. Could be them, but I ain't never met a troll I liked, so could be any of 'em.'

★　★　★

As we rode, the weather changed—for the worse. Storm clouds rolled in from the mountains, and jags of lightning stabbed down at us. Then the rain came, dirty, gritty rain. Different to what I'd been used to on the eastern arm. Yenene said this kind of rain was caused by the fallout from the collapsed western arm.

We journeyed for hours, following the trail of hoof prints but saw nothing save a lone distant thunder dragon with its fearsome horned head, long scaly tail and wings that bore spear-sharp talons.

Finally the prairie came to an end, descending into a river valley of dense scrub and cactus. Tyrone said we'd be making ground on those low-belly varmints with every stride—even with their head start, driving the calves would keep the thieves to a slower pace than we could manage.

Still, it wasn't long until the light began to fade and the clouds darkened. Tyrone hollered for us to call it a day and we halted our horses in a grassy space among boulders and near a stream.

'We'll make camp here for the night,' Tyrone ordered.

I was surprised we were stopping. 'Won't the rustlers get away?'

He shook his head. 'They'll have to camp as well. If they drive the calves too hard without a break for the night, they'll be good as useless to them.'

Through the gloom I spotted a cool bubbling creek and I walked with Moonshine over to it.

'If there's a breed o' horse I hate it's them fat, smelly troll horses,' she complained. 'They got no respect, especially for sky-cavalry horses.'

'Ain't too fond of them—or their mounts, either, and I thought we'd 'a' caught up with them by now,' I confessed.

'I did too.' Shy bore her large front teeth. 'I plan to show 'em how a horse with sky-cavalry blood running through her veins ain't one to be messed with.'

I left Moonshine having a well-earned drink and returned to camp to help Tyrone build a fire. Then we heated Grandma's soup in a smoke-blackened iron cauldron.

Once we'd eaten, some of the men moved aside to set up a poker game, but I sat with the others talking. Well, I didn't really do much talking—they planned out how they would hang the rustlers from a tree branch for all to see when they caught them.

Pretty soon, the moon rose over the hills. I rolled out my bedroll, and, using Moonshine's saddle for a pillow, I lay down, hat and gun belt by my side. I was exhausted, but my mind was galloping. I thought about all kinds of stuff. I thought about Deadrock and what it must be like to be trapped inside that great underground city knowing you might never get out. Then I thought about Jez who might be crawling through the mine air vents by now to try and get medicines and supplies to the town. I hoped she was OK.

Tyrone must have been able to hear me tossing and turning and he came over and crouched beside me. 'Don't worry, we'll catch up with that rustling scum tomorrow, get those steers back to Phoenix Heights and your grandma where they belong. Our livelihood is on those hooves.'

The talk from the others round the fire had bothered me. 'What will you do to them when we catch them?'

'You know me, Will, being a peaceful sort, my view is that the jailhouse is plenty punishment for thieves. Still, there are a lot of folk reckon that if any thief deserved to swing from a noose then it'd definitely

51

be a cattle rustler.'

In my book, Tyrone was right. The rustlers hadn't murdered anybody—being stuck behind bars was probably plenty punishment for them. 'Where do you reckon they're headed?'

'Most likely edge bound, out to Stoneforest. If they are snake-bellies they won't wanna be away from cover of a dark cave for too long in case this mist lifts.'

Troll eyes are sensitive to sunlight—Mid-Rock City trolls sleep all day then make a racket during the night while other folk are tucked up in bed.

'Stoneforest, that's the place Grandma told me to keep away from when we moved up here—think she'd read stuff about it in the paper.'

'You'd be right to listen to her; Stoneforest is a dark evil town. I was there recently seeing if I could source supplies for the ranch but I swore I'd never go back. Just like its name it's a forest sort of place, lying at the foot of the Edge Mountains, only it's made of stone. Trolls who left the western arm and Deadrock, and some from Mid-Rock City too have carved a bit of a town there. Trolls like it cos it's dark and gloomy on account of all the shadows. Sky cavalry are afraid to go anywhere near it cos of the lookouts in the taller front rocks at the entrance to the town.'

'Don't like the sound of it.'

He rose and tousled my hair. 'Should get some shut eye—could be a long ride tomorrow. Good night, Will. And don't worry, we won't be following the rusters into that evil town.'

'G'night, Ty.'

★   ★   ★

I woke at dawn to find a roaring fire going again and Tyrone cooking breakfast. He handed me mine: waffles, bacon, fried bread and a mug of coffee. I hadn't slept well for dreaming about Stoneforest, and finding myself wondering what the rustlers would be up to, but I told Ty I'd slept just fine and wandered over to see Moonshine as soon as I'd finished eating.

'Hey, Shy. You sleep OK?'

'Like a foal with a full belly.'

'Speaking of which—you eaten yet?'

'Ty gave us all some hay, though don't smell as good as that fried bread y'all were crunchin'.'

I took out a piece from my pocket. 'Hmm, good job I saved you a bit, then!'

She devoured it then whickered. 'You reckon we'll catch them rustlers today?'

'We got to, Shy. I ain't up for another whole day in the saddle and no result.'

★　★　★

Once all the men had eaten, we rode out again. It was frustrating for me and Shy as we continued to keep the horses grounded. It was still too misty to fly and we needed to be sure the trail of troll horse prints really did lead to Stoneforest.

We rode through deep gullies cutting across a range of low hills until one of the front riders shouted, 'Woah! We gotta turn round. Everybody backtrack.'

I wasn't far behind him. 'What is it?'

'It's a dead end, only way outta this gully's the way we rode into it.'

Tyrone groaned, along with most of the others, as the message made its way back to them, complaining, 'Gonna cost us valuable time and let the rustlers get even further ahead.'

I wondered about trying to find another way out when I spotted something on the ground. Wolf tracks! I warned the others: 'Keep your eyes peeled, there are fresh pick-tooth wolf prints here.'

'I'm enjoying this outing less and less,' Moonshine joked.

Tyrone rode up and squinted into the dirt. 'Heck, you're right, Will. Maybe it's a good thing we gotta ride straight back outta here. Don't wanna run into a pack o' those predators in a hurry.'

'You heard him—let's get outta here, Shy!' We and the other guys turned and rode back the way we came pretty sharpish.

As we approached the crest of a low ridge Moonshine's ears suddenly pricked up, and I soon spotted what had caught her attention. On the other side, far in the distance, I saw the Edge Mountains and at the foot I could just make out what appeared to be great columns of dark rock towering high into the sky. I felt a cold chill run down my neck.

'That the place you were talking about?' I asked Tyrone who was still riding alongside me.

'That's it, all right, that's Stoneforest. It—'

'Wow, look there!' I suddenly spied the dust of a herd on the move. I blinked, scarcely able to believe my eyes—it was *our* herd! I recognised the brand instantly—I'd branded them myself only a couple o' days ago.

And, amid the dust, I saw the rustlers too. Four horses, mounted by four trolls clad in black, knee-length topcoats with wide-brimmed hats and shouldering big rifles.

'There's the rustling scum!' I yelled.

'That's them, all right,' Tyrone cried,

waving an arm to the men behind us. 'Let's go!'

I didn't need to spur Moonshine into action as she galloped off with the others down the slope towards the rustlers, flexing out her wings.

'Don't worry, Will, I ain't taking off, just doing a wing spread.'

'That the thing your pa taught you?'

'Yeah, it's a sky-cavalry tactic to make the horses look bigger and more imposing to the enemy.'

'Good job, Moonshine.'

I needed to look scary to the enemy too. Unholstering my six-shot I let off a couple of rounds into the air. I'd not shot a gun many times, preferring my blowgun or bow and arrow—elf weapons. The noise was deafening.

The trolls broke away from the herd and steered their mounts towards us, opening fire.

'Yaaa! Yaaa!' I cried, not because Moonshine needed goading onwards but cos Tyrone yelled at us to make as much noise as possible. I fired a couple more bullets into the clouds. Moonshine kept up her wing display, letting the trolls know that we could take to the sky at any moment where we'd rain down more gunfire on them from above. It seemed to work and two of the trolls pulled up their mounts then turned round to gallop off. The other rustlers yelled curses at them though, and continued to ride at us.

'Keep it up, men!' Tyrone cried. 'I think the stupid trolls have figured they're outnumbered.'

The remaining trolls fired a few more half-hearted rounds before they too began to pull up their horses. The rustlers scattered, no longer bothered about the herd just worried about saving their own necks.

As they fled, some of our ranchers aimed rifles behind them, firing blindly. Others made to gallop after the rustlers, eager to catch them and hang them all from a high tree branch—just like they'd talked about last night.

But Tyrone yelled, 'Let them go!'

'What? But we could catch 'em, boss—hang 'em!'

'Yeah, it's only what they got coming to them.'

'I said, let them go!' Ty repeated. 'We got the calves back, and aside from us all being bone weary and a bit saddle sore from the day's riding, we ain't lost anything.'

I could tell by the expressions on some of the ranchers' faces they disagreed with Tyrone and were reluctant to let the rustlers go.

Tyrone rode past me. 'Good job, Will. You too, Moonshine. Now, let's make a start rounding up them frightened young steers and driving 'em back to the ranch before they decide to make a break down the valley.'

'Where the trolls headed?' I asked as I rode towards the calves.

'Not sure, but probably Stoneforest just like we figured, it's that direction they fled in. Just as well we caught up with them when we did—we definitely couldn't have followed them in there.'

With so many of us, we rounded up the calves easily then prepared to set a trail for home.

As we started out, Moonshine and me riding 'point'—up front with the lead steer—I glanced back at Stoneforest, the tall thin towers of dark gloomy granite clumped together like trees, and again I felt another cold chill run up my spine.

Moonshine felt it too, and shook out her mane. 'Glad we're heading 'way from that spooky place right now. Not sure any number o' missing calves would have got me in there.'

★   ★   ★

The ride back to Silver Brook didn't seem to take as long as the journey out, and soon we were re-uniting the calves with the rest of the herd.

I was in no rush to return to the ranch. Somehow, after the excitement of chasing rustlers, mucking out the stable or other ranch chores back at Phoenix Heights didn't sound so great.

So Moonshine and I took it easy, talking as we went.

'That's the first time I been in a fight with rustlers,' Shy commented.

'Yeah, it sure got scary back there when the bullets were flying. You kept a cool head, Shy. I was proud of you.'

'Got my pa to thank for that, and the good sky-cavalry blood he had in him. Which reminds me, Will—you know that horse years are about five times that of human years, or elf years for that matter?'

'Yeah, I heard that somewhere.' I smirked, curious to know where Shy was going with this.

'Well, it's just I ain't gettin' any younger and I wondered, what with Jez enlisting into the sky cavalry that maybe you'd think 'bout taking the plunge yourself.'

'You're talking like an old lady there, Shy,' I laughed. 'You got years yet.' But I knew she was serious. 'Jez mentioned 'bout me joining the cavalry too, but I ain't sure.'

'Why not?'

'I got a lot on my plate with the ranch and thinking about Uncle Crazy Wolf and what he could teach me, not sure I could factor in joining the sky cavalry on top of it all.'

'But you'd be a natural. It's just as much in you as it is in me, I know it is.'

'Shy, it's kind of you to talk that way, and to be honest with you it's on my mind more than it was before Jez joined, but like I say there's just so much going on round here.'

We were a little way out from the ranch now and I became aware of the raised voices of the other ranchers. I glanced at Tyrone, who was calling to the men, his voice full of urgency. Trying to work out what the problem was I saw that the rancher pointed up ahead. My eyes raked the prairie in the direction of Tyrone's finger until I saw it.

Smoke! Distant plumes of grey smoke spiralling like a tornado to join the grey mist in the sky.

'What is it?' I asked, catching up to him.

'Probably a brush fire,' Tyrone explained. 'Been a lot of lightning around of late. We should get a move on.'

But his expression told me there was something more troubling him.

'What's up, Ty? If it's a brush fire, it'll just burn itself out, right?'

'Brush fires can spread rapidly and are a real danger, especially when they're near towns and cities—and I hate to say it but I reckon it can't be far off from where we're headed.'

'What? You mean it's near Phoenix Heights?'

'Hope I'm wrong but it looks headed that way. I think it's time we took the horses to the air.'

A stone lump rose in my throat. Grandma was back at the ranch! What if something awful had happened to her? What if the wildfire engulfed Phoenix Heights and she couldn't get out in time? Thoughts of the way we'd been bickering of late over elf magic made me feel even worse. We couldn't afford to waste a minute.

'Shy, y'hear we gotta go up? You OK?' I called, spurring Moonshine onto a full gallop.

'Am I OK? Are you kidding? If it's to check on Grandma I'm more than OK, let's go!'

The horses were tired after the long trail, and the weather was still far from ideal for flying but this was an emergency and Moonshine and the other horses were highly trained. Without a murmur we soared into the air; Tyrone and the others flying alongside us into the misty sky.

But all too soon my worst nightmare slowly appeared out of the mist. As we flew closer to the ranch I saw that the nearby woodland remained untouched, the surrounding brush was as green as we'd left it. This was no brush fire.

I yelled at the others. 'It's the ranch house that's ablaze!'

Chapter Four
★
Inferno

Tears welled in my eyes as I spurred Moonshine lower, towards the blazing ranch.

'The whole place is engulfed by flames,' I cried. 'I just can't believe it, Shy!'

'We gotta stay calm. Whatever's happened, I'm sure Grandma is OK, cavalry-horse instinct. Now let's get down there.'

It was like a terrible nightmare, except in nightmares you don't taste the thick acrid smoke on your tongue; don't cough and feel sick to your stomach. No this was real— very real. I fought to keep a cool head, like Moonshine had said, and get down there fast. I had to find Grandma amidst that inferno. She would normally be having her afternoon nap around this time. What if she'd been asleep when

67

the fire had started and couldn't get out?

Even in my panic I wondered how it could have started. Grandma was so careful where fire was concerned; she'd never leave the stove unattended if she was cooking stuff, although she had been a bit distracted of late. And what about Rusty who'd stayed behind nursing his broken leg?

Soaring nearer, I saw that not only was the ranch house blazing but the barn and all the outbuildings were alight too. I felt a knot of bile rise from my guts.

'Not too close, Will!' Tyrone yelled. 'Bring the horses down at the arch entrance.'

I raised my hand in acknowledgment and steered Moonshine lower to land near the wooden arch—probably the only thing that wasn't on fire in the whole ranch.

'Stay here, Shy. I'm going in there!'

'I'll take you, we'll ride over.'

Tyrone overheard me and rode to block our path. 'No, Will, you can't. It's far too dangerous.'

'But Grandma could be still in there.'

'We don't know that for sure. Maybe she rode into town for those supplies she was making a list of before we headed out. I've despatched a few men to check the surrounding area and see if they can spot her. You go anywhere near that inferno you'll be dead meat for sure, and your grandma will probably ride up to news that her grandson's been cooked inside the ranch house.'

As Tyrone was speaking, I noticed that one of the ranchers who'd just set off to check the surrounding area had dismounted and was shouting and waving to get our attention. *Grandma?!* We raced over. But it wasn't Yenene; Rusty lay on the ground, his crutches strewn nearby. His bloodied face was paler than a mine wraith and sodden with sweat.

Dismounting, Tyrone and I crouched beside him. 'Rusty, are you OK?'

'A few cuts and grazes but I'll live, just lucky I paid a visit to the outhouse when I did otherwise I'd be dead meat.'

'What happened?'

'Snake-bellied trolls—three o' them—rode in on black mounts and torched the place. They were dressed in black with wide-brimmed hats, even their mounts were black . . . Yenene's gone.'

'Snake-bellies?!' I gasped furiously. 'And they took Grandma?'

He nodded, fear flashing in his eyes. 'They went inside and must've ransacked the place judging by the noise of stuff crashing about . . . it was like they were looking for something. Then they came back out with a struggling Yenene, bound and gagged.

It was then I saw the flames upstairs.'

'They took her alive?' Despite the sick feeling in my belly, I was relieved at this.

'Yeah. I managed to get the rifle—the one round the back of the outhouse Yenene keeps hidden for emergencies—to try and fend them off, but my stupid ol' crutch snapped and I fell in a heap . . .' Rusty paused and shuddered. 'They were riding out of here when the big troll, who looked like the leader, looked back and I caught a glimpse of his face for the first time. Gave me chills it did, I ain't seen anything like it before . . .'

'Like what?' I urged.

'His eyes weren't normal. They were like pools o' red fire glowing in his eye sockets.'

I shivered. Who was this troll, their leader? And were there any guarantees he wouldn't kill Grandma?

Moonshine rubbed her head against me reassuringly as I caught sight of the smoke belching out of my room and thought of my belongings; my bed, and fishing stuff, and those missing elf-

It was then I saw the flames upstairs. The...... Despite the

magic books—all of it up in smoke.

I couldn't understand why this was happening. 'What do trolls want with Grandma?'

Tyrone frowned. 'I agree, it don't make sense. What could they want with an old woman who keeps herself to herself?'

I sighed, pursing my lips. 'Place is gonna burn to the ground. I feel so helpless. What can I do?'

'Nothing, now just stay put.'

Just then I heard the sound of bells clanging in the distance and a loud whistle. I turned in the direction of the noise to see a horse-drawn, red-wheeled fire truck tearing along the dusty track towards Phoenix Heights. The truck was manned by five firemen in dark-coloured uniforms, wearing

leather helmets that had long neck brims. Two men rode up front while the rest sat on the wagon beside the big steam pump with its brass boiler and shiny copper funnel that belched out great puffs of steam. An array of smaller cylinders, pipes and rolled-up hoses adorned the rear of the truck.

They drew near the front of the blazing ranch. The chief approached us while the other men immediately got to work unravelling hoses and starting the pump.

'What happened?' The chief shouted over the roar of the flames.

'Snake-belly scum torched the place, kidnapped the elderly lady owner,' Tyrone replied. 'We just got back from chasing rustlers to find the whole place up in flames.'

The firemen directed jets of water, waving their hoses back and forth over the front of the ranch house; they moved forward, into the flames like soldiers advancing into battle. And the fire was the enemy, seeking to destroy anything that got in its path.

I helped the firemen at the truck keep the hose straight.

'Who called you?' I asked.

'Sky cowboy on his way to the city, flew nearby your ranch and saw the blaze. Whole rock's gone crazy, if you ask me.'

'What do you mean?'

'Past month's been the worst I seen for fires and lootings—last week an entire goblin village was burned to the ground out by the Edge Mountains.'

'Who do you reckon's responsible?'

'Dunno, but they need to catch 'em soon or the West Rock is gonna descend into lawlessness.'

I shuddered. How in the world was Grandma caught up in all this?

The firemen fought the blaze long and valiantly, and soon the flames died back and the sodden charred ranch house, or what was left of it, smoked and smouldered under the grey clouds.

I wanted to ride straight to the High Sheriff and tell him what had happened, hope he'd call out the sky cavalry to chase after the trolls.

Looking at the wreck, I couldn't hold it in anymore and sobbed into the palms of my hands. Tyrone put a stocky arm round me.

'Ain't said to you before, Tyrone, but something's been troubling my grandma of late. She wouldn't tell me what it was, or she'd make excuses or tell me some old story to shut me up but I knew she wasn't telling me everything—holding something back. Bugs me when I think about it now. Could be somethin' serious.'

'You know, now you mention it, Will, I kinda noticed she ain't been herself recently. Guess I put it down to the stress of the move and all the extra work.'

'I'm gonna ride Moonshine over to Fort Mordecai to tell the High Sheriff. Will you keep an eye on the herd and things?'

'Don't worry, Will. You go do what ya gotta do, me and the boys'll stay right here and look after things.'

I shook Tyrone's hand. Not only was he was a great ranch foreman but he was a good friend.

★   ★   ★

I landed Moonshine at dusk on the outskirts of Mid-Rock City then found a trough of water for her after the

77

flight before we rode on into town.

Mid-Rock City was, as always, full of activity. Stagecoaches and wagons trundled noisily along the dusty streets past hotels, stores and saloons fronted by wooden-planked walkways.

As we trotted down the main street a lone horseman rode up alongside us. 'Hey, kid. Those are some mighty big ears ya got below that cowboy hat,' he sneered. 'Ain't it time you were riding back to Gung-Choux Village.'

I was used to this sort of attitude in the city. 'If it's any of your business I'm a rancher from the mid-rock.'

'A half-breed rancher, eh? Now that's gotta be rarer than a friendly troll.'

I felt Moonshine bristle. I hated that expression, 'half breed'. No matter how many times I heard it, it made me feel like I didn't properly belong anywhere. But I didn't have time for this now. I knew I belonged with Yenene and I had to keep focused on getting her back.

'So long, mister. Both halves o' me happen to be in a hurry.' I squeezed my heels, urging Moonshine into a canter.

Glancing back I noticed Shy swish her tail in annoyance at the rider's horse as we hurried on through town towards Fort Mordecai.

Soon we passed Mid-Rock City graveyard, or the 'Bone Orchard' as folks call it. Posters had been nailed to the perimeter fence:

It made me think about Jez and her mission to Deadrock. Hopefully she'd already be back safe—I might even see her in the fort.

The fort was an imposing sight—rectangular and made of solid, half-metre-thick timber; surrounded by a deep ditch with sharp, wooden spikes protruding from it. At each corner there stood lofted lookout towers, where a cavalryman wearing a neat blue and yellow uniform and carrying a rifle was on guard.

As we climbed the rise to it, I quickly became aware that a noisy crowd had gathered at the fort entrance. Riding closer, I could see that the mob, consisting mainly of troll folk, was staging a protest rally, like Jez had mentioned.

'Wow, look at the crowds,' said Moonshine, pricking up her ears. 'What's that they're shouting?'

Riding closer I could make out the gruff-sounding troll voices chanting: *'Free Deadrock now! Free Deadrock*

now! Free Deadrock now!'

'They're protesting that the High Sheriff should be doing more to free the trapped folk of Deadrock,' I explained. 'It's what Jez was saying the other day at the ranch. They just don't get it, Shy. The High Sheriff has a duty of care towards his men, and if he reckons it's too dangerous to excavate the rock and dig out the tunnel to Deadrock then they gotta accept it.'

When I'd been here before, the fort had lain open with a sentry posted at the front gate but this time the solid timber gate was firmly shut.

I sighed. 'Looks like the fort's closed for business.'

'Maybe they're afraid of the protesters storming the gates,' Shy commented.

'Well, it don't look like we got much chance of anyone opening the gate to us, even if we did manage to fight our way through that crowd of angry trolls.'

'So what's the call?'

'We'll go and see Uncle Crazy Wolf

at Gung-Choux Village. He should be told what's happened to his sister. And he's a skilled tracker—he'll know how to find her, I'm sure of it.'

Moonshine nodded. 'Eastern arm here we come!'

83

Chapter Five
★
Gung-Choux Village

Tirelessly, Moonshine soared below a dark cloudy sky. Near the edge of the mid-rock, far below on the ground, I spotted the blackened, burnt-out shells of broken stone and timber that had once been a village. I'd seen too much destroyed by fire today. Feeling a lump swell in my throat, I thought of what the fire chief had said about that goblin village. This was nowhere near the Edge Mountains so it couldn't be the one he'd mentioned. But he was right, the rock sure was becoming a dangerous and lawless place to live.

We flew on down the side of the mid-rock to the eastern arm, my mind running over and over the events of the past few days, trying to make sense of them. It was a long flight but as it was all descent Moonshine was able to soar a lot, so it wasn't too tiring on her wings.

She'd had a busy couple of days.

Soon I saw the giant totem pole and colourful tepees of Gung-Choux Village. I breathed a sigh of relief; they were all very much as I'd left them. Landing just outside the village, we set off at a lope through them all, heading for the middle.

The big central totem pole was a breathtaking structure, made up of man-height sections placed one on top of each other, each section painstakingly carved in the shape of an animal native to the West Rock: an eagle, a frog, a pick-tooth wolf and, at the top, the head and spread wings of a mighty thunder dragon, which always filled me with a sense of awe.

At the foot of the totem pole I saw the elf drummer, his bare chest covered in paint, sitting by his two large painted, skin-covered drums. The elf drummer is the most muscular elf in the village, built up from beating the enormous drums with heavy club-like sticks that I could hardly lift let alone play the drums with.

'Woha, Roaring Dragon. You take

long time to come visit but it is good to see you.'

'You too. I wish I was here in better circumstances but I have bad news for my uncle, is he around?'

The big elf extended a tree-trunk arm in the direction of a cluster of elf homes. 'In his tepee.'

Dismounting, I gave Moonshine a pat on the nose. 'Go get a cool drink, Shy, you deserve it after that long flight.'

Arriving at my uncle's tepee, I entered the flap door.

'Woha, Uncle Crazy Wolf.' I said in greeting.

'Will! You have come—what a welcome surprise.' He looked up from where he sat by the fire, watching a pot of water he was bringing to the boil, a smile across his face. Bare-chested, his green skin was painted with magic symbols in bold yellows and reds. He wore fringed buck-hide leggings decorated with colourful beadwork. On his head, over his grey hair, was a band with a single feather that rose skyward like his long pointy ears. His face was

adorned with the two parallel white stripes that denoted a medicine mage.

Sinking to my knees by the fire, I blurted out the news. 'Uncle Crazy Wolf, Grandma is missing—there's been a fire, a terrible fire!'

He stared at me, wide-eyed. 'Wait, wait, Will, slow down a bit now. A fire—where?'

'Back at the ranch house; it's burned to the ground. I'd ridden after a posse of rustlers with Ty and the men, almost as far as the rock's edge, then when we came back the whole ranch was ablaze. Firemen put it out but Yenene's gone. One of the ranch hands who'd stayed behind saw three trolls on black mounts ride up, kidnap Yenene then torch the place.'

'This is grave news indeed. But why do such a thing? They must have had a reason for taking her.'

'I just can't work it out. And I feel terrible about it, as before she went missing we had a bit of a row. She's been acting strange of late.'

'Acting strange, in what way?'

'It's hard to explain, it's just little things, really. She's gotten real jumpy and wants me to wear this all the time.' I showed him the scorpion pendant.

My uncle recognised it immediately. 'That old thing? She wore it all the time when we were younger—never quite understood why she loved it so much.'

'And she seemed funny when Jez

89

was talking about trolls the other day. There was something weird about Grandma's reaction when she heard the name Jake Sixsnakes—did she know him?'

'I don't think so. Never heard of him myself, who is he?'

'Snake-bellied troll who's apparently set himself up as troll leader and voice against the sky cavalry. He's organising protest rallies over the poor treatment of the folk of Deadrock.'

'This is all news to me, Will, and I don't like the sound of any of it,' said Crazy Wolf. 'But I think it is very suspicious that the rustlers lured away you and all the ranchers.'

'Lured away? What do you mean?'

'I mean, what if the rustlers had no interest in taking the cattle, what if it was just a diversion to get you all away from the ranch?'

'Of course!' The rustlers had given up the calves easily once we caught up to them. 'So they might be working for this Sixsnakes fella too? Then if we were to pick up the trail of rustlers again, it might take us to Yenene.'

'It's the only lead we've got so it's definitely worth a try.'

I brushed away thoughts of those dark gloomy towers. I had to find Grandma. 'We should ride to the valley near Stoneforest, pick up the trail of the rustlers where we left off this morning and see where it leads us.'

Crazy Wolf glanced upwards to where the night sky was visible through the chimney at the conical point of his tepee. 'Too dark to fly now, we'll head first thing in the morning.'

Chapter Six

★

Stoneforest

The next morning, after breakfast, Moonshine flew me and my uncle back to the top of the West Rock. None of us said very much—even Shy was quiet. I guess we were all still in shock over everything that had happened.

We flew above Silver Brook, heading for the place I'd encountered the cattle rustlers. When it got too misty to fly, we rode across those low hills cut through by deep gullies with little vegetation, then across open prairie, descending into a river valley of dense scrub and cactuses. I hadn't thought I'd be back here so soon.

Finally, we spotted the trail over the rise and followed the prints of the fleeing rustlers.

I clasped the scorpion pendant in my hand and for a moment I could

92

feel Grandma's grip around my wrist, hear the words she'd spoken so firmly, *'Put it on, Will. I want you to promise me that you'll never take it off. It's more important now than ever. Do you hear me?'*

What was it all about?

I wondered what sort of night she'd put in. I worried those snake-bellies might hurt her, but I couldn't bear to think about that so quickly put it out of my head. Would she be frightened in the company of the trolls? I'd never really seen Grandma frightened much, she was always so strong. It was easy to forget she was getting on for eighty years old. The big question was still— why had they taken her?

'Shy, what do you think them trolls would want with Grandma?' I asked again.

'I wish I knew,' she replied. 'I been thinkin' 'bout it for hours now, it just don't make any sense. I get shirty with my own shadow at times, but Yenene, she ain't got a quarrel with anyone.'

'You're right, Shy. She's stubborn as anything, but

everyone likes her—she ain't the type to have enemies.'

'Kinda spooky too, what Rusty said about the big troll's eyes being like pools o' red fire glowing in his eye sockets.'

I felt Moonshine shudder and gave her a reassuring pat on the neck. 'Don't worry, Shy, Uncle Crazy Wolf's gonna teach me elf magic again, ain't ya?' I said determinedly turning my head slightly to where my uncle was listening behind me. 'Every spare minute, as we ride, as we walk, I want you to teach me. Reckon if we're gonna have any chance of getting Grandma back then Roaring Dragon's gonna have to start doing some roaring.'

Where he held on, Uncle Crazy Wolf gave my waist a squeeze. 'I will, Roaring Dragon—I promise.'

Soon the sky darkened even more, and the faint misty shadow of the Edge Mountains loomed on the horizon. A storm had settled over them—I'd heard it was a permanent storm that never stopped raging. At the foot of the mountains, those now-familiar tall, thin

slabs of black granite towered into the sky, tightly grouped together like trees in a forest. I felt the hairs on my neck stand up and a frost-cold chill run down my spine.

'Stoneforest,' I breathed.

We followed the trail of rustler hoof prints closer, and I saw that the stones were carved up by gullies, with barely a stagecoach width between them. A dark shadowy place, I reckoned there wouldn't be much daylight filtering down to ground level, which would suit the troll occupants just fine.

'Tyrone was right,' I said desperately. 'Looks like the rustlers might be *from* Stoneforest.'

Crazy Wolf shuddered. 'Why couldn't they been from Edgewater or Mid-Rock City? This place gives me the creeps.'

'You 'n' me both, Crazy Wolf.' The tall stones cast long shadows like fingers reaching towards us, almost pulling us in. I noticed Moonshine seemed to be deliberately avoiding trotting inside the shadows like even she was a bit spooked by them.

'It's OK, Shy. They're just shadows,' I said. 'But I know they're kinda freaky.'

She gave a nervous whinny. 'If the shadows are freaky, what's the place that's making them like?'

We were almost upon the gloomy town when I saw that the top of one of the entrance stones was shaped like a skull; sunken caverns near the top gave the impression of grisly orbits, while two smaller caves just below had the appearance of nostrils—a gaping mouth-like shadow finished off the gruesome likeness. My heartbeat quickened.

'You sure this is a good idea?' Moonshine asked.

'We gotta find Grandma, Shy. We'll be OK. If we can survive Deadrock we can survive anywhere.'

Part of me was real troubled, though. Deadrock was a dangerous place, no doubt about it, but Stoneforest seemed to ooze evil in a way I'd never felt there. Just looking at it gave me shivers.

'Ever get the feeling you're being watched?' said Crazy Wolf thoughtfully.

I frowned. 'The big skull rock?'

His forearm extended over my shoulder and he pointed to halfway up the entrance edifices. Suddenly I spotted what he was pointing to. Lookout caverns hewn into the rock. I saw figures—trolls—perched inside them shouldering enormous rifles, eyes raking the terrain. Why had they held their fire? Maybe as it was still daylight they couldn't see us too well. Or maybe they didn't consider an elf kid and his elderly uncle any kind of threat so were prepared to let us proceed.

The stones were even taller once you got up close to them. Towering over us, they seemed to scrape the sky. We headed past a cluster of real trees into a dark gully between a clump of entrance rocks. And entered the scariest town I'd ever seen.

Caverns both natural and troll-made had been hewn into the structures at ground level, and there were dwellings, stores, and other buildings, much like any other town. The narrow gullies between the rock structures formed a sort of road network dissecting the town, and horses, carts and stagecoaches careered along them much too fast, making it a hazardous place to explore on foot. There was no doubt about it: Stoneforest was scary but it was also probably the most breathtaking town on the West Rock.

'We've come to the end of the trail, Will,' said Crazy Wolf.

'Yeah, now we gotta follow our instinct to find Grandma. What sorta places would rustlers hang out in?'

We passed all types of establishment: mercantile store, gunsmith's, undertaker's, hotel, and then we came to a saloon.

The sign above the swing doors creaked in the breeze. On it was a picture of a snarling pick-tooth wolf baring dagger-sharp

teeth, drooling great gobbets of saliva. Underneath, in blood-red lettering, it read: *The Panting Wolf Saloon.*

I shuddered. 'Could be a good place to start? Somebody might talk.'

'A barrel of some of the rottenest apples on the West Rock,' my uncle stated. 'I've read about this place in the *Mid-Rock City Times*. We'll need to keep our wits about us if we want to get out of here in one piece.'

We dismounted. 'You be OK out here, Shy?' I asked.

Moonshine gave a swish of her tail. 'I'll keep my eyes peeled for those rustlers or for any sign o' Grandma.'

Inside, the saloon was overcrowded and bustling with activity. I could feel eyes on us as we cut a trail through the thick bacca-weed smoke, past a tinkling piano to the long wooden bar then squeezed up to the counter between two foul-smelling, burly trolls. After a while the barman, a snake-belly with forearms thicker than Moonshine's neck, trudged over.

'Whattayawant?' he growled rudely. Why would anyone want to order anything from him? Then he burped loudly and began drumming his stubby fingers on the bar counter. 'Well? Ain't got all day.'

'I'd like a bottle of Boggart's Breath and two glasses, please,' Crazy Wolf ordered. I must have looked as confused as I felt cos he turned to me, adding, 'Don't worry, Will, I haven't suddenly taken to strong liquor—the whiskey is for bargaining not drinking.'

He took the glasses and made for some tables at the back of the saloon. I went to follow him but as I reached for the bottle, long fingers shot out and grabbed my wrist.

I looked up. 'Ain't seen ya around these parts, boy,' snarled the wart-infested goblin now holding me in a handcuff-tight grip.

'We're just passin' through,' was the best I could come up with.

It obviously wasn't enough to satisfy the inquisitive whip-tail.

He shot a glance at my ears. 'Most elves pass *by* this town not through it. What makes *you* so gutsy? Reckon

you're better than us folk, don't ya? I can tell by the look of ya.'

The goblin had a chip on his shoulder the size of a fence plank, and he was itching for a fight.

'Never said I was better than anyone.'

Uncle Crazy Wolf re-appeared to clasp a hand round my captor's arm, and the goblin let out a wail, releasing me. Cursing, he blew on the singed material of his smouldering shirt sleeve. 'What the . . .?'

I recognised the magic immediately and was stirred by my uncle's skilful use of it in a crisis. I was embarrassed all over again at my own faltering attempts at magic in the stable with the wraith.

'Kid ain't worth botherin' yerself about, pardner. We ain't lookin' fer trouble.' Uncle Crazy Wolf fixed the goblin with a steel-eyed stare, murmuring in his normal voice, 'Bring the Boggart's Breath, Will. I think I might've spotted a patron willing to trade some information for liquor.'

As he ushered me away from the bar counter I cried, 'Where'd you learn to ranch-speak like that? You sounded like a hardened sky cowboy there— mean one too!'

'Just picked it up.' He grinned. 'I've always wanted to do that.'

We headed over to a back table with a lone troll and an empty glass at it. As we approached, his eyes fixed on our whiskey, and he licked his lips.

Crazy Wolf set down the bottle. 'Can you help us? My sister's missing. Think some trolls from round these parts might have had something to do with it.'

'Well, seeing as you gents are stupid enough to wanna part with a nice big bottle of Boggart's Breath, I can tell yez that Jake Sixsnakes got a finger in most pies where this town's concerned. So if ya reckon yer missing sister is around here then he's the troll ya should be talking to.'

Jake Sixsnakes! The name hit me like a punch on the nose. He was the troll who'd been organising the protest rallies to free the Deadrock folk and who Grandma seemed to know, given the weird way she'd reacted when Jez had mentioned his name. And now it seemed he was big news in the place we thought Yenene had been brought to. He sounded like an evil critter but he must be able to give us some information about where Grandma might be.

'Where can we find this Sixsnakes?'

'Ah, now that's the key. Don't be thinking yer just gonna be able to walk straight up to him, or that he's gonna wanna talk to ya. But, as yer about to leave town, there's a peak known as Bighorn Rock, ya won't miss it. Sixsnakes got his cronies guarding the place so ya ain't putting a boot to the bottom step without him knowing yer comin'.'

'One last thing,' I tried.

The troll eyed the bottle. 'I'm kinda thirsty, what is it?'

'What's the deal with this Sixsnakes? He set himself up as some kind o' mayor o' this place?'

'S'right. Came outta nowhere few months back. Ain't seen much around town but he got influence. Oh, an' he's no ordinary troll, y'know, he's different.'

'What do you mean?'

He grinned. 'You'll see.'

We left the saloon. I was glad to get a proper lungful of air. 'It's a start,' I coughed to my uncle.

Moonshine whinnied from where she

stood waiting outside the hotel, and we started across the road to fetch her. But then I noticed she was frantically nodding her head, eyes like saucers and pawing the ground with her front hoof. She was trying to tell us something. Following her gaze, I quickly got the picture.

A gang of scowling whip-tail goblins was fast approaching from the doorway of the gunsmith's shop opposite, waving six-shot blasters. And one of them was the goblin from the saloon, his sleeve still bearing the charred burn marks from my uncle's magic.

'We'll never make it to Shy!' I cried.

'So where, then?'

I thought quickly. 'That stagecoach!'

Chasing after the passing coach, I grabbed the rear boot and hauled myself up. Crazy Wolf did the same and soon we were both grappling our way onto the roof. 'Follow us, Shy, but keep yourself at a safe distance. OK?' I called as we passed Moonshine.

'You bet. Don't worry none 'bout me.'

Glancing back I saw the goblins were

jeering in annoyance, chasing after us on foot. The warty goblin from the saloon fired his gun and I felt bullets whistling past my ears. Next thing he jumped onto a passing cart, snatching the reins before pushing the farmer into the dirt. This goblin was either easily annoyed, bored, very stupid, or all three, I thought; but one thing was for sure—he was determined.

I suddenly remembered I still had the gun Tyrone had given me when we went after the rustlers. I reached for it as I warned my uncle, 'We're being followed by a whip-tail.'

I saw that Uncle Crazy Wolf had already spotted them and had a windball half conjured in his hands; he was now lining up a shot at the cart.

I lined up my shot too and fired, waiting for the bang, but it must've been jammed as nothing at all happened. I threw it at the goblin in frustration. 'Stupid gun. I've got to get back to magic, Crazy Wolf—I feel useless.'

'Not useless, you're out of practice, that's all. And don't worry, when the time comes, I will deal with your grandma, she'll let you practise magic again—let us just find her first.'

Uncle Crazy Wolf fired the swirling ball of wind at the cart. But it whistled past its target, crashing into the window of a mercantile store.

'Not used to shooting on the move,' he shrugged, already crushing some dried leaves in his palms to try again.

'Get down from there, you crazy fools!' The stagecoach driver had spotted us now and was cursing and yelling at us to get off.

The second windball was a hit; it flew past the horse, and into one of the front wheels, which shattered, sending the cart crashing into the side of the road. The goblin tumbled to the ground, straight through a wooden barrier surrounding a gaping hole. He clung by his fingers, wailing pitifully.

We jumped off the coach, hearing the goblin scream as he lost his grip and fell to his doom. Carefully, we edged past the smashed barrier to peer down the hole into the blackness.

'Looks deep,' I said.

'I'd say we just shook off our whip tail.'

A drunk troll wandered past muttering. 'Another one, huh?' I heard him say. 'This town has got more holes in it than a pair o' moth-eaten socks.' We'd better watch our step here.

Up ahead I saw the streets widen and the big stone pillars start to thin out, it seemed a lot less populated too. 'We must be close to Jake's place. Didn't the troll in the saloon say it was on the edge of town?'

Crazy Wolf nodded as I heard a familiar neigh and looked round to see Moonshine galloping out of town to join us. We stood aside to let her in.

Just like the saloon troll had said, Bighorn Rock wasn't hard to spot and you didn't have to be a genius to see why they'd named it that; a tall, thick column of grey rock now stood in front of us, its summit features were two tapering peaks that looked like huge cattle horns. An arched entrance led inside to what must've been a natural cave. A wart-infested troll stood guard outside, shouldering a rifle. We'd

arrived at the abode of Jake Sixsnakes.

'Guard looks friendly,' Crazy Wolf grinned.

'If he smiled his warts would crack.'

'Do we have a plan?'

I tapped the jar of frog poison on my belt, then reached into my bag,

 removing the blowgun and dart.

'Of course.' My uncle nodded approval. 'Reckon he's not just gonna let two elves in to see his boss.'

'I just need to get a good shot on target and it's nighty-night, wartface.'

'Wait, look there!'

A group of about a half dozen, well-dressed trolls walked purposefully towards Bighorn Rock.

'Looks like Jake's expecting company,' I said.

Crazy Wolf nodded. 'Seems it is not only us who want to talk to him.'

'They look like city trolls—trolls that can afford fancy suits,' I observed. 'They're the ones Yenene said were worth the watching—she said they were even worse than gunslinger outlaw trolls.'

We watched the trolls approach the guard, who looked like he was expecting them. With a grunt he stepped aside allowing them to enter.

'Give it a minute, Will, then we'll dart our handsome friend and follow those trolls in,' said Crazy Wolf.

'What does a place like this say to you, Uncle Crazy Wolf? I mean, why would a troll live somewhere like this?'

'Eccentric? Perhaps insecure?'

'I'd say more like a swellhead. I reckon this Jake Sixsnakes thinks he's some kinda big shot,' I said as I aimed my blowgun.

My dart found a home in the neck of the guard and soon he slumped to the ground, snoring.

I gave Moonshine a pat on the neck and told her to wait for us then turned to Crazy Wolf. 'Let's go check out Bighorn Rock.'

My heart raced as we entered the cave with no idea what lay ahead. Still, there was no way I was going anywhere but forward. Grandma's life was at stake and I was determined to find her and bring her home.

Chapter Seven

★

Jake Sixsnakes

Inside Bighorn Rock, we made our way down a stony corridor to where the passageway widened into an enormous cavern. Pale purple light shone from thick saddlewood tree branches that stuck out of the cavern walls. My uncle ushered me towards a large boulder, a hiding place where we could watch what was happening.

The well-dressed posse of six trolls were clustered round a hooded figure—who I took to be Jake Sixsnakes—sitting on a stone throne in the middle of the shadowy cavern. Most of the trolls had uneasy expressions on their faces. I soon saw why.

Jake Sixsnakes was, like our friend from the saloon had told us, no ordinary troll, if he was troll at all. As he stood up I caught a glimpse of his face beneath the hood for the

113

first time—it was a pale white skull. He had no eyes, instead each orbit burned with a red glow.

Fear and anger welled up inside me. This *had* to be the same troll that Rusty had seen, the leader of the group who'd taken Grandma and then set the ranch house ablaze. I glanced at his hand; bone fingers curled round the handle of a gnarled wooden walking stick. Both scabbard and holster hung from his belt, housing a curved sword and gun. I felt my heartbeat quicken and a cold chill run down my neck. Jake Sixsnakes was a *skeleton*. He had no flesh that I could see, yet he lived. What kind of creature was he? I thought I'd come across every type of folk on the rock but I sure hadn't seen anything like Jake. Even my pa hadn't told me such creatures existed.

'That's him,' I whispered. 'The low-belly scum that took Grandma and fired the ranch.'

Crazy Wolf nodded. 'I fear it is. We need to tread carefully, like a lizard on hot Wasteland sands.' Then he blinked and drew back from me, pointing to the pendant around my neck. I glanced down and saw that the embalmed scorpion had started to glow red, not unlike Jake's eyes.

I gasped, lifting it away from my chest to examine it. It felt warm against my fingers. 'What's happening? I never saw it do this in all the years I had it.'

Crazy Wolf whispered, 'Nor I, even when my sister wore it as a young girl. We'll figure it out, but for now slip it under your shirt in case the light should give us away.'

Jake addressed the gathering, his voice was high-pitched and rasping like the last gasps of a dying man—or troll.

'So you found my humble abode? Well met, gentlemen, and I appreciate your coming.'

The troll party murmured greetings then stood quietly facing their host.

'The time has come for trolls of the West Rock to take a stand. Your families and friends have been left to rot to death in Deadrock, trapped in what will soon become their tomb. The sky cavalry have no notion of tunnelling them to freedom. You seen how when we offered to help they shut us out, that's because they want them all to die, the fewer trolls on the rock the better, they believe. Are you happy to let the sky cavalry treat our kin folk like this?'

Some of the trolls shook their heads, muttering to one another. I swallowed a stone lump. The vents were prone to collapse, and even though Jez was an expert at crawling through them it just took one rock quake and she'd be trapped down there along with the rest of the folk. I hoped again that she'd already been there and back.

The conversation continued. 'We're listening,' said the tall troll.

Jake went on. 'Too long have trolls been holed up in the belly of the West Rock or some cavernous town like this one, breathing stale air, labelled as outlaws or thieves, while the other rock folk strut about the rock-tops in their big boots, out in the open, living off the fat of the land: grazing cattle, growing crops. It is an outrage, gentlemen, and I've invited you here today to ask for your support—along with the trolls you represent—in the war against the sky cavalry.'

'Sixsnakes' words gotta a ring o' truth 'bout them,' said one member of the party.

'Yeah,' agreed another.

The tall troll edged forward, and his voice quivered slightly as he replied, 'Name's Punk, and I agree somethin' needs to be done—like ya say, the High Sheriff has gone too far this time.'

Another fat troll in the group stepped towards Jake, his brow furrowed, 'I got me some concerns.'

'Concerns,' Jake hissed. 'What concerns?'

'I'd like to know more 'bout who we'd be fightin' alongside. Yer proposal—taking on the mighty sky cavalry—sounds pretty dangerous.'

'You will fight alongside other trolls. My warriors are trolls and I am a troll.'

'*You're* a troll?' He looked unconvinced. 'Ya talk about breathin' stale air but I reckon y' ain't breathed any sort o' air, let alone stale air, in a long time.'

Jake stood up and, using the cane,

limped over to the fat troll till he was barely centimetres from his face. He clenched his skull teeth together making a snarling noise, and the skulls of his belly snakes appeared from beneath his cloak, their eye sockets glowing red too. The fat one cringed away, but I agreed with him, Jake sure wasn't the kind of troll I was used to seeing about the rock.

'What's the matter, do my bones offend you?'

Punk elbowed his reluctant neighbour. 'Troll might be a skeleton, Hegg Grumill, but he's got more guts than you, an' you got a big fat belly full o' them!'

The other trolls roared with laughter, even Jake sniggered, his bones rattling.

But Hegg wasn't finished, and when the laughter died down he asked, 'And where are your "warriors"? So far, all I seen is a big lummox of a guard at the entrance to this place.'

'For now my warriors sell bread and serve Boggart's Breath whiskey in town but at my command will take up rifles and saddle horses to ride with me in conquest.' As Jake spoke he waved over to a dim corner of the cavern where slatted boxes were stacked high—I was sure I could make out rows of shiny wooden rifle stocks jutting from the tops of some of them.

I nudged Crazy Wolf. 'Rifles. Must be a hundred,' I breathed.

'At least,' he replied with a shudder.

'I like what I hear,' Punk asserted, 'and I'm pretty sure I can persuade twenty or thirty trolls to join me back where I come from.'

'Your bravery impresses me. And I welcome your support.'

A few of the others indicated that they too were willing to join Jake's revolt against the sky cavalry.

Punk asked, 'What plans you got for the High Sheriff?'

'Simple. I plan to kill the High Sheriff—and every soldier in his precious sky cavalry. I alone shall be ruler of the West Rock.'

'And what about the rest of us— those of us here who will support you?'

'You shall have a seat on my

120

council; a position of great honour and importance. I hand-picked you as men of influence and wisdom on the rock, and you can be sure your allegiance will not go without generous reward.'

I heard a noise behind us. Turning, I realised it was the big ugly troll I'd darted outside. He was awake and presumably coming to look for whoever had knocked him out.

'We'll have to move,' I whispered. 'There's no way we can approach Jake anyway, so maybe we can take a look around, see if we can find Grandma. She could be in here. All this seems linked to Jake.'

'You're right. Where to, then? We can't go back that way.'

'That tunnel leading off the main cavern—d'ya think we could make it without being spotted?'

'Yes, if we keep low and stay close to the boulders for cover.'

I could hear the footsteps of the troll getting closer and his curses.

121

'C'mon, let's go.'

Hardly daring to breathe, we scuttled like river crabs behind the boulders, edging towards the small tunnel. It was dark, which made it difficult to see my footing, and I stumbled a couple of times, making more noise than I wanted to, heart in my mouth. But Jake was locked in conversation with the troll posse, and by the sound of the cheers it seemed he was winning their support to smash Fort Mordecai and kill the High Sheriff. My guts churned, the future for Jez looked hopeless— whether she was still in Deadrock or back at Fort Mordecai. And, of course, there was Grandma. What had this evil skeleton monster done with her? Was she somewhere inside Bighorn Rock? If he was so cold and calculated about killing the High Sheriff he'd surely have no mercy with an old elf woman. But what had he come all the way out to Phoenix Heights to get her for?

As we disappeared inside the tunnel, we heard Jake bawl at the troll guard, asking him why he was staggering about, and saying that if he was drunk he'd kill him. Then we heard the troll protesting, telling Jake to be wary of intruders in the cavern. I took that as a cue to get moving a bit quicker along the dark tunnel.

Crazy Wolf conjured a little ball of glowing light that floated from his hands to hover above his shoulder. The magic completed, he blew what looked like crushed leaves off his palm.

'I sure hope Grandma is somewhere down here.'

'I pray we will not only find my sister but another way out too.'

By the light of the magic I peered up ahead. The tunnel had come to an end and darkness gaped. I took out my blowgun. It was all I had now—I'd thrown Tyrone's gun at the goblin.

'Looks like another cavern,' I said. 'I think we could be inside the smaller pinnacle, the one with the little horn on top.'

'The Little Bighorn.' Crazy Wolf grinned.

'There's no saddlewood here. Maybe it's Jake's sleeping quarters. That's if skeleton-trolls, or whatever kind of evil

123

thing he is, actually sleep.'

'Your pendant, is it still glowing?' Crazy Wolf asked. 'It worries me.'

I slipped it out of my shirt, feeling my fingers tingle as I touched it. I was certain I could feel something now, seeping from deep within the amber resin into my fingers. It reminded me of the tingling feeling I used to get in my palms when I conjured a fire ball (before I got so out of practice); a feeling of power yet at the same time of being protected from the scorching flame, a feeling of magic.

'It's glowing, only more dimly. And I think I can sense magic from it. What could it mean?'

Crazy Wolf frowned. 'It is indeed magic, I sense it too, but a magic I am unfamiliar with. Quick, we must hurry and find a way out—I'm sure that troll guard will come poking his warty nose about down here before too long.'

Checking behind to make sure he hadn't followed us, we split up, exploring the cavern. The light ball followed my uncle and not me so it was hard to see. I felt my way round

124

the craggy walls, hoping to find an exit tunnel when my hand brushed something propped against the wall that moved as I touched it. I felt about—it was a long wooden pole. Carefully, I stepped past it. If it was some sort of support beam the last thing I needed was the roof caving in on us. I continued on my way when suddenly Crazy Wolf yelled, 'Will, stop!'

'Wha—?!'

'Don't take another step.'

Crazy Wolf sent the ball of light shooting through the air towards me, revealing a huge hole extending across from my feet to where he stood. It was much bigger than any of the naturally formed holes I'd seen so far in Stoneforest, and one that would have swallowed me up to my doom.

I heaved a huge sigh of relief. 'Thanks, Uncle Crazy Wolf, you just saved my life.'

He didn't answer.

'Crazy Wolf? You OK?'

'Look, Will!' He seemed to be staring at something behind me.

I turned to see that the wall there had been painted with chilling symbols in red and black: an oval shape with teeth like a gaping mouth, crisscrossing lightning jags below a cloud, an eye shape with an arrow through it and others. I'd never seen anything like them before.

'What are they?'

'Dark-magic symbols,' Crazy Wolf said fearfully. 'But I don't understand what they're doing here. They must be affecting your pendant somehow.'

I felt frightened and bemused at the same time—trolls and magic didn't normally go together, so what were dark-magic symbols doing on a troll cave wall?

126

Just then I heard a muffled noise. It was strangely familiar and seemed to be coming from inside the hole. Looking over the abyss, I could see nothing in the gloom. I heard the noise again and tensed. It was a voice. The troll guard? No, it wasn't gruff enough, it was fearful, pleading.

I looked up and saw something move above the hole towards the cavern roof. My first thought was that it was stykes—the living stalactite creatures I'd encountered in Deadrock. They're evil critters that cling to the roof of caves waiting for a passer-by to unwittingly walk below them; then they fall from the roof and skewer you, feasting on your flesh—with tiny saw-sharp teeth. But stykes are quiet, except when they are stripping a dust rat of its flesh after they've speared it, that is. 'Crazy Wolf, can you send the light ball up to the roof?' I asked. 'I can hear something.'

Crazy Wolf sent the light skyward and as it rose it illuminated not a styke but a thick strand of rope running vertically from the cavern roof right down into the hole. Somebody was in there!

'Who's there?' I cried.

More muffled noises.

My gaze followed the rope's course back upwards from the hole to a pulley wheel then along the roof of the cavern and down the cave wall where it coiled around a wooden barrel with a lever. I guessed that turning the lever by hand would raise or lower whatever the rope was tied to and I hurried over to examine it more closely.

'Someone's down in that hole!' I cried. 'Quick, Crazy Wolf, give me a hand.'

My uncle grabbed the handle with me and together we turned it. The pulley wheel squeaked through lack of a good oiling and the rope stretched taut as slowly we reeled it in. The grunting noises grew louder.

A net appeared from the hole, made of thick rope. And inside the net, gagged with a bandanna pulled tight through her teeth, hunched and holding her knees was a wizened old elf woman—Yenene.

Our loud gasps echoed round the cavern.

'Grandma! Thank the spirits, you're alive.'

'My sister!' Crazy Wolf cried. 'So now we're sure Jake was responsible for torching the ranch and kidnapping her.'

Grandma struggled inside the net, desperate to get free, her eyes wide and darting wildly between me and Crazy Wolf. She made all manner of noises and grunts through the gag, though I couldn't understand a word of it.

'Hold still, Grandma, we'll get ya out o' there in no time.'

'How we going to do it?' wondered Crazy Wolf. 'Lowering this will just lower her deeper into the hole.'

Suddenly I remembered the wooden pole I'd brushed past earlier.

'Uncle Crazy Wolf, can you direct the light ball to follow me?' I said, hurrying to the cavern wall. He did as I asked and I was happy to see my hunch was right—what I had disturbed earlier was not a roof support but a long wooden pole with a hooked end.

'Reckon Jake must have used this to grab the empty net over to the edge, bundle Grandma inside then push her out over the hole to leave her hanging there.'

Crazy Wolf frowned. 'But why?'

'Cos he's a twisted weirdo who thinks he can take over the rock.'

'But I don't see where an almost eighty-year-old elf woman fits into all this.'

'I'm sure once we get that gag off her mouth we'll find out.'

I thrust the hooked end out towards Grandma, but just as I did so, the darkness flashed and a shot rang out, ricocheting around the cavern. There was a stench of gunpowder and the sound of dragging footsteps mingled with the tap tap of a walking cane.

Then a voice came, 'Either I've got an infestation of squeaking dust rats or somebody's turning my pulley.'

And two red eyes stared out of the gloom.

It was Jake Sixsnakes.

'Well now, whom do I have the

pleasure?' He pointed a gun at us. 'Wait, don't tell me, let me work it out.'

His head turned and red eyes burned first into Crazy Wolf. 'Another ancient elf—perhaps the child from the village all those years ago. The magic is strong in you, old timer, I get the feeling I shall have to keep my eye on you.' As he spoke one of his glowing orbits expanded fleetingly.

'What sort of dark creature, are you? Troll or skeleton?' spat Crazy Wolf.

'Oh, I'm all troll, though I confess I've lost a little weight since those village days. I am also the future leader of the West Rock so you will address me with a little more respect.'

Jake wasn't making any sense. He sure didn't look like any troll I'd come across, and what did he mean about Crazy Wolf being a child from the village?

He turned to me, his skeleton belly snakes hissing and snapping. 'And the boy fisherman, I'm especially glad to have reeled *you* in.'

'Fisherman?' I was livid but I wanted answers.

'I searched your room before I set fire to it; I saw the fishing rod and tackle.'

'Then it *was* you who destroyed my home!'

'Who else? I made it obvious enough, didn't exactly cover my tracks.' And he laughed defiantly. 'With the help of my rustler friends making sure we were uninterrupted.'

'You're scum, Sixsnakes,' I fumed. 'And I can see why you got no flesh— you'd be a waste o' any good skin that covered those evil bones. Why'd you do it?'

'I was looking for something, well two things, really. This wizened old woman with whom I have a score to settle, and for the object she stole from me.'

I felt my chest burning, and glancing down saw that the pendant was glowing brighter than ever. I could sense its magic even more forcefully now, giving me strength, while at the same time making me feel less fearful.

'Ah! What have we here?' Jake seemed to have fixed it with a red-eyed glare. 'The pendant is glowing like that because it is *mine*. Your thieving little grandma here stole it from me many years ago. I kidnapped and have been holding her until she told me its whereabouts but now *you've* gone and delivered it straight to me.' His jaw locked in a skull-toothed grin. 'You probably didn't know she was a thief.

In fact, there's probably a whole lot about your beloved grandma you don't know. You probably don't know she's a murderer too!'

'Never!' I shot back, fists clenched as I noticed Yenene shaking her head vigorously inside the net. 'You're a rotten liar. My grandma is no murderer and no thief, either.'

I went for Jake but he thrust the barrel of the gun directly at me. 'Temper, temper.'

Crazy Wolf grabbed my arm to calm me down. 'As the brother of the one you tell lies about, I can assure you my sister is none of those things.'

'How would *you* know? You were only a blubbering little baby sitting in your own poo. I hope you're a better mage than your mother—mind you, it would be hard to be any worse.'

'You knew my mother, Little Phoenix?'

'Till your sister killed her, yes. Imagine killing your own mother—*your* mother, wizard man. Doesn't that make you hate her?'

'Troll scum!' Crazy Wolf bellowed.

135

Now it was my turn to restrain Uncle Crazy Wolf as Jake swung the gun at him.

'Seems you both have a lot to learn about my captive here.' He pulled the rope to make the net swing and Yenene gave a muffled cry, eyes downcast. 'Give me the pendant!'

'Let her go!' I cried.

'The pendant first.'

'Why?'

He pointed the gun at me again. 'Don't play games with me, boy. Give me that pendant or I'll splatter your brains all over the cavern!'

Grandma's words about me never taking it off echoed inside my head, but, fingers trembling, I removed my hat and slipped the pendant from my neck. 'It's magic, isn't it? But what do you want it for?'

Sixsnakes strode a few paces towards me then stopped suddenly, his cane quivering in his hand. 'Because it contains something very precious, something belonging to me . . . Do you know what kind of scorpion is in the pendant?'

'It's a bloodsucking scorpion—they used to crawl all over the western arm before it collapsed.'

'Very good. You're not as stupid as you look. So now maybe you can guess what it is the scorpion possesses of mine?'

I frowned. What could a scorpion take from anybody? They were small little critters and couldn't carry anything heavy in their tiny pincers. It dawned slowly on me that it wasn't anything the scorpion had carried, it was what it had ingested.

'You . . . your blood?'

There was something about the way Jake was keeping his distance from me that seemed odd. He could've shot me then limped over and ripped his precious blood-filled pendant from me at anytime but he hadn't. Why?

With the pendant in my grasp I became even more aware of the intensifying magic coming from within the glowing amber, of its power—but of something else too . . .

I decided to try something and, very slowly, I held the pendant out to Jake.

137

'Come and get it, then,' I said.

'Toss it over to me, elf boy.'

'And risk it falling in the hole?' I went on. 'Take it—it'd be much safer.' Jake took a step back.

I saw my uncle's quizzical look and whispered, 'The pendant *is* magic, maybe even dark magic. But I think Jake's lying—it ain't his, it's maybe got something to do with him but it ain't his. The magic is circling me. I've got a hunch that for whatever reason the pendant protects the wearer—me—from him!'

'Which would explain why he's shirking in the corner of the cavern.' Crazy Wolf gasped, then with a howl of delight he stared at Jake. 'You can't touch it, can you? Not while it's in the hand of another.'

'Curse you, curse you both!' Jake boomed. 'Stop playing games. Give it to me now.'

'Would also explain why you want it so much,' I went on. 'So you can take on the sky cavalry.'

'You think you're so clever, but you're way off, boy.'

Crazy Wolf must have had some more dried leaves with him as suddenly I noticed a thunder ball growing in his hands. A thunder ball is similar to a wind ball, only a more powerful, more destructive type of magic. Moments later, he cast it directly at Jake. Not expecting it, as it careered into the skeleton-troll's ribcage it sent him hurtling backwards across the cavern— he lost his grip on the gun and landed roughly on the rocky ground near the pulley wheel.

Jake laughed loudly, slowly getting up and dusting himself down. He left the cane lying at his feet. 'That was pitiful. I can see you *are* almost as hopeless a mage as your mother.'

I gasped, terrified at how Jake could be so unharmed by my uncle's powerful magic.

I heard Crazy Wolf muttering the spell to conjure a fireball this time but Jake, in a lightning move, unsheathed his sword and sliced through the rope that held Yenene.

'No!' I cried. But he held fast with his other hand above the cut so the net didn't drop.

'Direct your pathetic magic against me again, and I let go of the rope. Give me the pendant and she lives.'

'You're asking a lot for us to believe that once you've got the pendant you won't just let go of the rope anyway,' said Crazy Wolf.

'The pendant is all I want,' Jake hissed. 'You can keep the elf hag.'

Yenene was going hoarse with grunting, eyes blinking, she was shaking her head frantically. What was going on? What was she trying to tell me?

'Give it to me now!' he rasped, and he let go of the rope. The net lurched down towards the hole, my heart with it, as Yenene let out a gagged cry.

'Nooooo!'

But with another lightning move Jake caught the rope again, the net stopping just level with the edge of the hole.

'Now!' he shouted.

I looked at my uncle, his expression was solemn. 'I fear, Will, that we have little choice. I do not condone what evil he has planned with the pendant but my sister's, your grandma's, life is at stake.'

'You could say it *hangs by a thread*,' Jake added with a sneer. 'I'd listen to your uncle, half breed.'

I stared down at the pendant. The scorpion seemed to glow an even deeper red, it felt heavier too. Magic oozed from the oval of amber, I could sense it. My gaze shot between Jake's red orbits to Grandma then my uncle. Finally, reluctantly, I tossed the pendant to Jake.

141

It fell in the dirt in front of him and the skull of a belly snake flashed in the dim light as it shot down to snatch the cord between its fangs then coiled back up to Jake, who took it with his bony fingers. The villain threw back his head and let out a triumphant gasp, belly snakes hissing loudly, writhing excitedly. The pendant glowed brighter than earlier as Jake clasped his hand tight around it. The other hand kept hold of the rope. So far he'd kept his word.

'Now give us the rope.'

The troll didn't answer, his head still thrown back as if he was in some kind of trance-like state, oblivious to us.

At first I'd been so focused on the hand that Jake held the rope with that I didn't notice what was happening to the other, the one which grasped the pendant. The red glow was intense and from within it red tendrils suddenly sprang up between his fingers and began latching onto pieces of bone, knitting together. The tendrils ran the length of each finger then spread up over his hand bones. Around the red light, flesh appeared, starting at the finger tips and moving up his body like a macabre flesh glove that was pulling itself on. But it didn't stop at the wrist. More threads of tissue appeared above Jake's shirt collar, writhing around his neck bones and onto his skull, coiling around the jawbone as he began to make ghastly gurgling noises mixed with laughter. Horrible grinning teeth were now veiled in sneering lips, a fat warty nose formed over nostril holes, and orbits were clothed in eyelids, though when they opened I saw that the eyes themselves still glowed red.

A couple of belly snakes appeared from below his shirt but weirdly I noticed *they* were still skeletons. Why hadn't they grown flesh? Whatever the reason, they didn't seem too pleased and snapped their pin-sharp teeth and fangs at me with even more venom.

Heart hammering, I stared at the snake-bellied troll then gasped, 'Reckon he was a lot better looking when he was a skeleton!'

What kind of dark monster was this? Whatever, he held Grandma's life by a thread of rope.

When he spoke, Jake's voice was different, lower, gruffer, brimming with power. 'Y'know, scorpions always did make my skin crawl,' he roared and kicked the walking cane at his feet into the hole. Then he burst into uncontrollable laughter, coughing and spluttering.

Catching his breath, he fished a bottle of Boggart's Breath whiskey from his coat and, pulling off the top with his teeth, took a long swig. When he'd finished he gasped loudly, wiping his mouth with his sleeve. 'Ah, that liquor sure tastes good after nearly seventy years.'

He walked to the edge of the hole still clutching the rope and faced Yenene who shook violently. I'd never seen her looking so vulnerable.

When he spoke again Jake's voice was chilling. 'The last time you looked into this face you dragged me by a rope and tipped me like some worm-ridden animal carcass down a hole. Now it is I who holds the rope, and it is you who shall fall down the hole. You

should curse the day the western arm collapsed—it gave me my freedom. Goodbye, Yenene!'

And, expressionless, he let go of the rope.

The net and my grandma plunged into the hole.

'Nooooooooooooooooo!' Tears filled my eyes, blurring the surroundings into a purple haze. I felt crushed. I'd come so close to rescuing her but had failed. I heard Jake laugh madly, then to my horror I saw a fire ball swirl out of nothingness above his newly skinned palms, growing bigger than any I'd ever seen, and burning ferociously. I glanced at the dark-magic symbols on the wall again as it hit me like a steam train at full throttle—Jake could do magic, serious magic. But how? A troll wielding such skill was unheard of on the rock.

Fixing us with a red-eyed scowl he prepared to unleash the fire ball at us. Fear gripped me and my head swam. I felt cornered and frightened, like a trapped wolf facing death by a wolfer. My legs felt like they were turning to butter—I thought they might give way. Then I felt my uncle's great hand clasp my upper arm as he drew near. 'C'mon, Will. I think it's time we got out of here.'

'But . . . where do we go?'

'Trust me.'

And linking his arm tight to mine, he dragged me forward and we fell headlong into the hole.

Chapter Eight

★

Little Phoenix

Numb with fear, my guts jumped into my throat as I fell through the blackness.

Had my uncle chosen this over a blazing troll fireball?

In the midst of the total horror of tumbling to my certain death I was suddenly aware of a loud rush of wind shooting down the gulf below us, illuminating the darkness in an expanse of swirling grey and blue light. Crazy Wolf had somehow managed to conjure a massive wind ball as he fell, sending it hurtling down the hole.

The great ball of glowing magic disappeared, and darkness once again filled the hole. I was conscious of a distant crashing sound, like when a tornado first rips into a piece of woodland or an outbuilding. Then I heard a low rumble, getting gradually louder. I felt cold air gusting into my

body, stronger and stronger. Blue light flickered below as the wind ball reappeared, surging up from the depths of the abyss, illuminating the craggy walls of the hole that sped past me.

As it approached I was sure I spotted a sprawled figure, clothes billowing, at the centre of the wind being carried up towards me. It looked like Grandma.

Moments later a wall of air slammed into my body as I was engulfed by the wind ball. The walls of the hole no longer sped past me, and I could

pick out detail, crags and outcrops—
I even thought I saw a styke. I was still
falling only much slower now.

But the noise was deafening. Hat
long gone, my hair blew wildly and
my cheeks felt like they were trying to
climb off my face. I heard someone
shouting and saw Crazy Wolf was
beside me, grey hair billowing. He was
like a soaring eagle the way he was
able to move an arm or a leg to change
direction. He drew alongside me as
I looked down and saw that I hadn't
imagined my earlier vision, Grandma
was falling below us, still gagged and
bound.

Crazy Wolf pointed down then
slammed his fist into his hand
repeatedly, which I took to mean
we were close to the bottom. Maybe
he'd worked it out by how quickly the
thunderball had struck the base of
the hole before bouncing back up. I
thought about how craggy and uneven
the ground had been in Bighorn Rock
and started to panic. The wind ball had
slowed us a fair bit but we were still
travelling pretty fast. It was gonna be a

tough landing.

My uncle was performing more air acrobatics and, linking my arm somehow, caused us to swoop lower so he could grab Yenene's arm too until all three of us fell together.

But the magic was beginning to fizzle out. It had carried us safely for a great distance, but wind-ball magic only lasts for a certain length of time. Thankfully it didn't matter as seconds later we arrived unceremoniously at the bottom of the hole and plunged into deep, ice-cold water.

Every nerve-ending on my skin screamed in shock as I held my breath, arms flailing in the water. I opened my eyes to see that Crazy Wolf's light ball had followed me underwater and now illuminated the surroundings. To my horror I saw Yenene sink deeper close by me, hands tied (which wouldn't have made much difference as she couldn't swim). Fighting against the freezing water I swam to her aid only to spot Crazy Wolf do the same thing. One of her thrashing arms came up and gave me a thump on the nose as I tried to grab her; I felt a wave of pain and saw a thread of blood spiral upwards past my eyes. Ignoring it for now, I managed to grab hold of her. Crazy Wolf lifted her from the other side, and somehow we managed to bring her to the surface. The light ball shot out of the water and hovered above us.

'Over there, Will, I think I see dry land!'

We swam to the bank, my arm under Yenene's chin to keep her head above the water. I climbed up first then helped Crazy Wolf to get Grandma out, laying her on the flat rock. Panting heavily, I extended a hand for my uncle to drag himself out of the water.

Behind him I saw my hat float over to me. Amazed, I fished it out and put it back on my head where it belonged.

'How'd you know the wind ball idea would work?' I gasped, pinching my nose to try and stop the bleeding from

Grandma's whack.

'Didn't, but we were dead anyway so I figured it was worth a shot.'

Yenene grunted. '*Mffffff!*'

'I think she wants her gag off.' Uncle Crazy Wolf smiled.

I untied the knot of the bandanna and freed Yenene's tongue for the first time in two days.

'Fools!' she yelled, almost spitting the gag from her mouth. 'Do you have any idea what you have done? You should've saved your magic, brother. Better we had all dashed our heads on the pool bottom than live.' And she began to sob bitterly.

My jaw dropped. I had never seen Grandma in this sort of state before, and I stared at Crazy Wolf who put a comforting arm round her. 'You must try and be calm, sister, and tell us what is going on. Whatever has happened we will find a way through, the Great Spirit will guide us.'

She was trembling but it was from more than just the cold, I knew, and when she looked up her eyes were sunken and wide and staring.

She shook her head. 'Even the Great Spirit can't help us now. The nightmare that is Jake Sixsnakes has come back, just like he swore to me he would. I can't believe it. I was stupid to hope he'd be gone for ever. I kept wanting the past to go away, I wanted it to have all been a nightmare but it's real— Jake's real. And the pendant, I . . . I can't believe you just gave it to him!'

'What is it with the pendant, Grandma?' I asked, untying her hands. 'I know it gave him his ugly face back, but there's more, isn't there? Why is it so powerful?'

She shuddered. 'His power was all in that trickle of blood. Up there you saw nothing compared to what he'll now be capable of. Even the High Sheriff won't be able to stop him. Jake's determined to take over the rock just like he was over seventy years ago when I last saw him.'

'That's when you dragged him to a hole and tipped him in, ain't it?' I remembered Jake's venomous words before he'd let go of the rope. 'If you stopped him then, we can do it again.'

But she shook her head.

Waving his hands, Crazy Wolf directed the little light ball to skim round the large cavern and land on the ground in our midst. It spread over the rock then took on a slightly different form, little flames flickering upwards like a camp fire. My uncle had told me before that this light magic was a very subtle type of elf sorcery that would last for quite a long time.

'Nice touch,' I said.

But Crazy Wolf's gaze was fixed on his sister who took off her shawl and began drying it at the heat, hands trembling. 'Presently we will look for a way out, but for now, my sister, you must tell us what happened.'

Yenene breathed a deep sigh then spoke. 'Over seventy years ago, when I was a young girl of seven, we lived in Phoenix Creek elf village beside a forest near the edge of the western arm.'

'Isn't that where the old broken totem stump used to be near the woods?' I asked. 'I used to ride out there with Shy.'

She nodded. 'I lived with my mother and father and little brother, your uncle Crazy Wolf who was only a baby.'

Yenene's words were solemn but I still couldn't help grinning as a funny image of my uncle as a tiny gurgling baby floated into my head.

'A posse of trolls led by an ugly snake-belly called Jake Sixsnakes were over-running the rock. At first we were

safe from them, but then they started riding by, helping themselves to our crops and cattle and horses. Then, it was just now and again, no more than a nuisance, but when they started coming round more often it became something sinister . . . They killed my father for taking a stand during one raid—Jake conjured a fire ball that wiped him out. He was very powerful.'

'We saw him do magic,' I said. 'Right after he dropped you down the hole. I don't get it—whoever heard of a troll doing magic?'

'Jake Sixsnakes is not a troll,' Grandma said gravely. 'He is a rock demon. And his name is not Jake Sixsnakes—that was the name of the poor unfortunate he possessed, now dead.'

I gasped. I'd heard stuff about rock demons from my pa but he'd never seen one. I felt the hairs on my neck stand up as my grandma continued.

'A rock demon is a supernatural malevolent being. In their real form they're part human and part rock goat, but often they possess a living creature which they become bound to—flesh and bone—for ever.

'Back then, Jake was building a following of men, starting with the posse, but ultimately his goal was to raise an army and take over the entire West Rock.

'The village medicine mage in those days was Little Phoenix, my mother.'

Jake had revealed this earlier but it still made me gasp. 'I can't believe you never told me my great-grandma was a mage.'

'She never told me, either,' added Crazy Wolf.

Yenene shook her head. 'I told no one, my brother.'

I was getting more and more intrigued. 'Did she show you elf magic?'

'No, she was careful not to force magic on me, but secretly I think she would've liked me to follow in her footsteps—she would be proud of you,

Crazy Wolf. She knew I was young, and I never asked her to show me so she didn't. I did watch her, though, and she knew I watched her, and that was enough for her for the time being—she was wise, very wise. I remember being fascinated by the little pouches of herbs and books she kept in her tepee.

'She did teach me about Jake, though, and the more she told me the more nightmares I had. She told me how she knew he was an evil spirit—a rock demon from the lowest pit—as he had no heartbeat and because she could see his red eyes that he tried to hide behind a wide-brimmed hat. She said until he was defeated there would never be true peace on the rock.'

'I gotta feeling, Grandma, that finally we're gonna get to the bottom of why you're so against elf magic.'

She looked at me, her brow heavy, and she nodded and then went on, 'After the death of my father, Little Phoenix became preoccupied with trying to figure out how to defeat Jake. There were no Wynchester Demon Shot rifles in them days to snuff out his evil soul for good, so at first she studied books on demons and dark magic. She discovered that an inexperienced mage who'd been dabbling in dark magic must have summoned the rock demon by accident.'

I thought of the smelly wolfer, Imelda Hyde, an apprentice of Uncle Crazy Wolf's years ago who had shown a lot of promise till she began meddling with the darker side of magic when his back was turned.

Yenene went on, 'The books seemed to suggest that the only way to defeat a child of dark magic was to use dark magic against them. The chief and other mages from neighbouring villages warned her not to do it but she insisted she was strong-willed enough not to be swayed by the dark magic.

'She was wrong.

'All too quickly, the dark magic took a hold of her. In front of my eyes, I saw my happy, carefree, fresh-faced mother become a troubled, gaunt, grey-haired witch-like recluse.'

Crazy Wolf frowned. 'Many years ago, I heard of this happening to some of the mages in the Edge elf clans.'

'She became obsessed with defeating the demon. It was as though she herself became possessed. Her eyes sunken from sleeplessness, she moved to a small tepee on the edge of the village and never came out. I had to practically become a mother to your uncle Crazy Wolf, looking after him. I cooked all the meals, that's when Ma even bothered to eat something— as a result she became as thin as a reed. Her bony fingers would thumb through dark-magic books looking for the spell that might defeat the rock demon. And she would grow more and more deflated especially when she realised that the best she could probably do was to bind it, that's if she could even get close enough to hurl a magic lasso around Jake's body.

'Then one day something happened that sent her into fits of glee. During a raid, she noticed Jake curse and flick a blood-sucking scorpion off his neck. She was so excited, demented almost. She knew that to possess even a fraction of the demon's blood could be powerful—so when the posse had left, Little Phoenix ordered me to scrabble around in the dirt with her, searching for the dead scorpion that had bitten Jake. I found it. In the belly of the scorpion was a tiny bit of the rock demon's blood.

'Little Phoenix performed a dark-magic spell then placed the scorpion in amber to preserve it, later crafting it into a pendant. The pendant would protect the wearer against the demon completely, and so adding a leather thong, she wore it around her neck.

'She now had the power to confront Jake and bind him fast for ever. But the cost was great. She was only a shadow of her former self.

'That night there was a terrible storm with thunder and lightning. I was sleeping in mother's tepee. I had nightmares about Jake, his red eyes burning into my dreams, and I awoke to see my mother asleep opposite me wearing the scorpion pendant, of course. I knew that the pendant protected the wearer from the evil demon. Terrified by my nightmares, and afraid that Jake would come and get me; I got out of bed and slipped the pendant from my sleeping mother, putting it around my own neck. Then I crawled back into bed and fell asleep.'

I could see where this was going. No wonder Yenene felt so strongly 'bout elf magic. Look where it had left her family.

She continued. 'Just before dawn, Jake returned. My mother sprang out of bed like a wood panther, dressed and was out looking for Jake before I'd even rubbed the sleep from my eyes. She told me to stay in the tepee, but when she'd gone I followed her from a distance.

'The village braves took a stand with spears and bows and arrows.

'The trolls had guns—all noise and black powder and not as accurate as the guns today, but deadly just the same—Jake carried no gun but used powerful magic. The elf braves had no chance and were met with heavy losses. I still remember the smirk on Jake's face as he rode round the village like he owned the place.

'Then Little Phoenix appeared out of nowhere to face him, carrying her lasso and medicine-magic pouch; her face painted and grey locks blowing wildly in the storm. I remember it so vividly, great jags of lightning pulled her witch-like face from the gloom.

'Jake just laughed at her and began conjuring a massive fireball. "You come at me with rope? Do you think I am some dumb animal that can be roped?" he sneered.'

I gasped, 'Little Phoenix sure was fearless to face him like that.'

'She was indeed,' Crazy Wolf agreed, taking Yenene's hand. Grandma took it but continued, as if she had to spill out this secret that had been inside her for so many years.

'Cowering behind a rock near the well, I clutched the pendant, suddenly realising that I still wore it and that my mother had no idea she didn't—and at a time when she needed it more than ever. I wanted to rush over and give it to her but I was frozen with fear. My heart drummed inside my chest as I watched the horror unfold before my eyes. She started chanting a spell and spinning the lasso till it glowed blue, sparkling with pure elf magic—just like you would'a seen Crazy Wolf here do, Will. Then Little Phoenix unleashed the lasso at him. It was a good shot but the rock demon was far too quick and easily stepped out of the way. Though Ma wasn't wearing the pendant, Jake couldn't touch the rope, the magic in it was much too powerful; touch it and he'd have been as good as bound.'

Yenene's voice was low as anything, her eyes staring ahead like she was in a trance as she told us the end of her story. 'Little Phoenix spins her second lasso. Only one rope left—one more chance. I can't bear

165

to look. The demon chooses his moment, unleashing the fire ball at her, knocking her off her feet. Her shoulder ablaze, she rolls over the ground to extinguish the flames. It's then I see her expression of fear as she puts a hand to her neck, realising the pendant is gone. The rope, still charged with magic, falls to the ground just in front of the boulder I'm crouching behind. More uncontrollable laughter, and the demon strides towards her, easily stopping her attempts to direct a thunderball at him. He stands over her then pulls out the longest and deadliest-looking sword I've ever seen.

'And my feet are moving stealthily, my eyes darting between the rope, still tingling with magic, and my mother. I am aware that I am not making a sound—it's like I'm gliding over the ground—to this day I'm convinced this was Little Phoenix empowering me from where she lay staring into those red eyes . . . I lift the rope like I'd done it all my life and I spin it similarly. The demon raises an arm as I let fly the lasso and it snakes through the air, on target it seems but taking much too long and only coming down over Jake's head after he has thrust the sword venomously downwards.'

'No, not my great-grandma,' I cried. Though I already knew that her death had somethin' to do with Sixsnakes, hearing it filled me with fury all o'er again.

Crazy Wolf sobbed. 'The cold-blooded monster!'

It was as if Yenene couldn't even hear us. 'I quickly repeat the same spell my mother chanted many times when she was practising in the tepee:

'Hwan yakan wakipa hakin kaga!

'He stares at the pendant around my neck. But he is powerless to do anything . . .'

Finally Grandma stopped for breath and came out of her trance; she had tears in her eyes.

'His bound cries mingled with my mother's dying groans have haunted my dreams for all these years. I had thought it would be instant, that

Jake would freeze but he didn't. He glowered at me with those demon eyes, and the worst of evil filled my head— in those moments I went to a very dark place.

'He cried out, "I will return, young Yenene, and you will die!"

'But bound he was, and moments later his body petrified, his face frozen in a ruthless scowl that I've never forgotten.

'My hands were quaking, I tied the other end of the rope to my horse and dragged Jake to the well, secured the rope, making sure it was tight, then dumped him down the hole, in case the others came looking for him wondering what happened.

'And then I just slumped to the ground right there, shaking and terrified and crying, crying because my mother was gone. Though really she had ceased to be my mother the day she became obsessed with defeating Jake.'

'I still don't know why you didn't tell anyone,' Crazy Wolf asked. 'Especially me, when I was old enough to understand?'

'I was frightened. I felt guilty. I blamed myself for our mother's death. If I hadn't taken the pendant off her she'd have been protected. So I didn't tell anyone about it or what really happened that awful day. I just told them Little Phoenix had died at the hands of the trolls. Then I took you and moved to a tribe on the eastern arm, as far away as possible from those sad memories.'

'You weren't to blame, my sister,' said Crazy Wolf. 'You were only a child.'

Grandma exhaled a long breath of stale cavern air then looked at me. 'Do you see now, Will, why I am so against you learning elf magic? Medicine magic took everything from me.'

Closing my mouth, which had been gaping like a gutfish for most of her story, I swallowed a lump in my throat. 'I do, Grandma, but you gotta realise it was *dark* magic that caught a grip of Little Phoenix and that won't happen to me.'

'That's what Little Phoenix told

everyone, but it *did*—dark magic creeps up on you when you least expect it, like a goblin sneak thief.'

Now I knew the truth, I felt sorry for Grandma, losing her father and mother at the hands of Jake and his posse. I didn't blame her for hiding my magic books and all the other stuff— she was only trying to protect me. I couldn't believe what Jake'd done to my family and I was determined to escape this hole, track him down then snuff out his evil soul once and for all.

'So how'd Sixsnakes get out?' I asked. 'What did it have to do with the collapse of the western arm?'

'He told this to me himself as I hung above the hole in that awful net. The well I'd dragged him to—like our village—was on the edge of the rock. Shortly before the western arm collapsed last year great chunks of the edge were breaking away and one of the breaks exposed the old well. A strong gust of wind a few days later blew his evil ol' bones over the edge and to freedom.'

I shuddered at the thought of the

rock demon down there for all those years, his red eyes glowing in the dark and damp, plotting revenge on my grandma. 'So, Jake Sixsnakes's body rotted away down there in the well, which is why that ugly lookin' skeleton is what came out,' I realised.

'You'd be right, Will,' Yenene said. 'An ugly lookin' skeleton who then set his sights on searching for me, and for the pendant he knew would restore his body and power.'

'So he must have laid low for a while,' Crazy Wolf worked out. 'Then made his way to Stoneforest where he allied himself with that nasty bunch of snake-bellies, asserting himself as their leader, promising them a better life by leading a revolt against the sky cavalry.'

Grandma shook her head. 'I hate to think 'bout the damage he could do now he's up to full strength again. World's a very different place to the one he knew before—full of dangerous weapons, and more folk.'

'How did he find you?' I suddenly wondered.

171

'He was riding by the ranch one day when he spotted our new wooden sign.'
I pictured it:

Grandma's old fire was showing on her face again. 'If I hadn't been so stupid and put my name on that spirit-forsaken sign he'd probably have never found me.'

'You're not stupid, Grandma. I can't imagine how hard it must've been for you keeping all that in for over seventy years.'

Crazy Wolf put his arm round Yenene. 'My sister, no child should have to go through what you have—I feel much pain and sorrow for you and the burden you have carried for so long.'

'I knew I'd never forget that day but I thought that sometime I'd be able to at least get over it and put it behind me, but somehow I never could. And now it's all come back to haunt me.'

'We'll help you get over it, Grandma,' I said determinedly. 'We'll sort out Jake once and for all—for Little Phoenix, for your father and for you.'

Chapter Nine

★

Tunnel of Fears

We started out along the dark, twisting underground passages, climbing at first to a chamber full of jagged stalactites and stalagmites then entering a narrow tunnel which descended steeply. My belly started rumbling and I figured it would be around supper time outside and probably getting dark. I'd left the smouldering ruin of Phoenix Heights just yesterday afternoon though it felt like much longer. Delving into my pockets I found some dried beef strips I'd taken after breakfast back at my uncle's tepee and I shared them with Yenene and Crazy Wolf.

'You OK, Grandma?' I asked as I handed her the beef—she still looked pretty shook up after having to re-live her first encounter with Jake all those years ago.

She managed a half smile. 'I'm OK, Will—though I'd be a lot better if we

174

could figure a way outta this place.'

I agreed—I thought of Moonshine up there somewhere. I hoped she was keeping safe and out of the way. I turned to Crazy Wolf. 'We should stick together as much as possible. There's only one light ball so we need to watch each other's back for stykes or holes.'

In some places the tunnel grew so small that we had to crawl. I was cold and my clothes were still damp. And as the smothering rock closed in around me, I felt scared. Would we ever get out of here? Every now and then I thought I saw a glint of red up ahead in the gloom and Jake's horrible warty face swam towards me in my mind's eye.

I've invited you here today to ask for your support in the war against the sky cavalry.

I feared for the future of the West Rock. Jake's address to the other trolls had been a rousing one, and that was on top of what Yenene had told me about him, over-running the rock with a posse years ago, conjuring dark magic like shadow-casting and wraith-summoning.

I used to think nobody would be any match for the sky cavalry, but if by now Jake had convinced all the troll leaders to join him, with the powers he had, he could terrorise the rock. Never mind a posse, this time he'd have an army!

I had to get out of these never-ending caves and warn the High Sheriff about Jake.

Up ahead the tunnel narrowed even more and became almost impossible to negotiate. Crazy Wolf and I had to help Yenene down some of the bigger drops. I missed my rope, tied to Moonshine's saddle, it would've made things easier here.

We found ourselves in a larger cavern, like the one we'd first fallen into.

'Uh-oh, look up there!' Crazy Wolf directed the light upwards.

I gasped. 'Stykes. Whole clutch o' them, we gotta tread carefully.'

But I noticed that, as the glowing light ball zipped along, the little critters scuttled sideways on their stubby legs, clinging to the roof.

'I don't think the stykes like your light ball,' I remarked. 'They're moving out of the way into the shadows.'

'Good,' said Crazy Wolf. 'Then as long as we stick close to the light hopefully they'll not harm us.'

But no sooner had he spoken than a big styke, whether through hunger or bravado, launched itself from the roof. Its target—Yenene's back.

'Grandma!' I screamed and yanked her out of the way. The styke just missed her, crashing to the cave floor, shrieking, then its tapered, slimy body scurried off into the gloom.

'Thanks, Will.'

We made our way quickly across the cavern until Crazy Wolf held out an arm, signalling for us to stop.

'What is it?'

'We have a choice of exits.' He pointed to the row of gaping tunnels and holes of varying sizes.

'How 'bout the biggest one?' I suggested, picking the closest.

I entered the gaping oval tunnel first, but quickly realised something wasn't right. Illuminated by the light ball, the walls glowed a deep blood-red and underfoot it felt soft, not hard and rocky. It stank too—like the smell of a rotting carcass on a hot day. Trying not to breathe through my nose, I pressed my palm into the tunnel wall and gasped in revulsion, it felt warm and soft and wet, like placing your hand on a mass of slimy slugs. I spun round to see Crazy Wolf help Yenene—who must've stumbled—to her feet at the tunnel entrance. 'Stop! Don't come any further!' I yelled.

Crazy Wolf froze, holding his sister. 'What is it, Will?' They were just about to follow me inside.

'It's . . . it's this tunnel—something ain't right,'I stuttered. 'I'm coming out.'

I doubled back towards the exit, my heart pounding, as a low gurgling noise resonated from deep within the tunnel and a blast of stinking air caught my neck, making every hair stand on end.

To my horror, the roof of the exit began to descend slowly, the floor rising to meet it, and as they closed together I could just make out small ridges—like teeth.

This was no tunnel—it was a living creature and I'd walked into its great gaping mouth!

I saw Crazy Wolf and Yenene stare in at me—wide-eyed with fear.

'Spirits help us! Run, Will!' my uncle cried, his palms flashing with the beginnings of a fire ball.

But the gruesome mouth-parts came

179

together fast as sticky saliva dripped onto my head, running down my cheeks. I made a dive for the closing mouth but it shut tight and I hit the rock-hard stubby teeth painfully with my shoulder and was plunged into darkness.

I lay trembling with fear in the blackness, hearing only my heartbeat and the awful gurgling noises of whatever creature this was. I was waiting to be crushed by more huge teeth or swallowed whole to die slowly in its rancid stomach. I rubbed my hands together, trying to conjure a fire ball but it was pointless—I couldn't do it.

Then, the darkness shook, as with the stink of burning flesh, the creature gave a loud moan, opening its mouth a little. It was just wide enough! I scrabbled through the gap to freedom.

Crazy Wolf pulled me to my feet, hands still smoking from the fire ball he *had* been able to conjure.

'What kinda critter is that?' gasped Yenene as we darted down the next

biggest exit tunnel. 'I could only see its mouth, nothin' else!'

'I have no idea, but I reckon I was pretty close to being its lunch.' I was angry with myself that I hadn't been able to conjure the fire ball back there. Maybe I'd never be able to do magic again—maybe it was all a sign I shouldn't have even been learning it in the first place. Yenene was right, I should leave it well alone. This thought stung the most and made my heart sink almost into my boots.

Crazy Wolf glanced back nervously. 'I am certain I read of such a monster many years ago—I believe it might be called a ghole—a gruesome creature that, much like a styke, disguises itself as a natural cave feature in the hope of luring its prey inside that fearsome mouth. Let's keep on the move in case it's not a permanent fixture of that cavern but can move about too.'

We hurried down the tunnel, making sure it was made of rock and not flesh, but then I noticed the light ball was beginning to fade.

'The magic is dying.' Crazy Wolf noticed too. 'Soon, it will go out completely.'

'Can't you conjure another?' I asked.

'I have no more magic leaves.'

Great, I thought. It was one disaster after another. I'd escaped the living tunnel creature only to die in the darkness at the hands of a clutch of hungry stykes. We were OK now but for how long? As the light faded, so did any chance we had of finding a way out.

'How much time d'ya think we got till it disappears completely?' I asked Crazy Wolf.

'*SSshhhhh!*' he said, suddenly halting.

I stopped and stared at him as he put a finger to his lips.

'My sister, did you hear that?'

Yenene cocked her head to one side, listening intently. 'Yes. Yes I hear something—like voices.'

'I don't hear anything.' All I could hear was our breathing. I guess half-elf ears aren't as sensitive as full-elf ears. 'But I'd sure like to check 'em out. Where they coming from?'

'From the end of the passageway, c'mon.'

The stykes from the cavern had followed us and skittered across the roof, closing in; less annoyed now by the light ball as it lost its strength. If we couldn't see them then I didn't know how Crazy Wolf was going to be able to cast a fire ball in their direction.

Then my heart gave a leap. 'Look, I see faint light up ahead,' I gasped. 'It looks like moonlight, which fits—

reckon it would be around evening time on the outside. C'mon, we might justa found an exit.'

'Then perhaps it was not voices we heard but the wind.'

I squinted into the gloom behind us. I couldn't see much, but I could hear the sound of stumpy legs scrabbling closer. 'The stykes are gaining on us.'

The three of us made our way towards the light, which glowed brighter as we got closer, emerging from the tunnel onto a narrow ledge. Blinking, my eyes raked the enormous cavern below, lit not by moonlight but by huge, trunk-sized branches of glowing saddlewood. All my hope sank into my boots—we weren't outside at all.

Yenene felt the same. 'Ain't no moon. An' I ain't feeling any breeze. Where are we?'

Crazy Wolf stared. 'I . . . I do not know.'

I stared about me. Stalagmites and a snaking railway littered the cavern floor, and where the cave wall sloped to our left there stood tall skinny wooden buildings tightly packed together like elf-headdress feathers: a saloon, undertaker's, gunsmith, general store, bank and a hotel. Below the ridge we stood on, a track wound its way from the town into the cavern, deserted save for a few tired-looking troll folk. In the distance I could just make out more rail track and an old freight station. Suddenly I knew exactly where we were.

Heart racing, I gasped, 'Last time I was here a ghost friend of mine commented it was always night in this city—only there ain't no moonlight here, you can be sure o' that.'

Yenene stared at me. 'You talkin' 'bout them ghosts you told me you met in Deadrock?'

'Deadrock?!' Crazy Wolf's face drained of colour. 'Spirits alive! I never thought I would see the day . . .'

'Place is creepier than a bucket of spiders, that's for certain.' Yenene shuddered. 'You sure 'bout this, Will?'

'Believe me, I'm sure. We're in Deadrock all right—once seen never forgotten.'

She sighed. 'Just our luck to stumble

into dead-end Deadrock, where the only exit has been blocked by a rock slide.'

The light ball went out completely and I heard the stykes, close now. They weren't bothered by the dull saddlewood light of the enormous cavern and scuttled on gruesome oily limbs across the passageway straight for us. One crawling styke lashed out at my ankle and I gave it a kick, sending it skittering back into the tunnel.

I looked down from the ledge we stood on. 'We're higher than a barn up here; we'll kill or cripple ourselves if we jump.'

Yenene glanced back nervously at the advancing stykes. 'Reckon we ain't got much choice—either that or be skewered by these ugly things.'

Spotting a couple of neatly dressed trolls (which was pretty surprising in a gangster troll-hole like Deadrock) pass close by below us, I cried for help. 'Hey, you down there!'

The trolls glanced all around, everywhere but up.

'Up here! Ya deaf or stupid or

186

something?' Yenene yelled, stamping on the tapered head of a lunging styke.

This time the smaller troll looked up, taking off her hat—which looked like a sky-cavalry cap—as she did so. I saw a familiar-looking mop of tousled black hair and big eyes. It wasn't a troll at all . . .

'Jez!'

'Will?! Am I seeing things? Where the heck did you come from—a vent?'

'Sort of. Big one, I s'pose.'

'Who's that with you? Wow, Crazy Wolf,' she gasped craning her head to see better. 'And, Yenene! But what's going on?'

'Right now a great big clutch of stykes is what's going on. Could use a little help.'

The troll in the suit muttered something to Jez then removed a pistol from inside his jacket and offered it to her.

'This here's the mayor of Deadrock—he was just checkin' you're friends o' mine.' She tossed me the gun. 'Catch?'

I did, instantly turning round and

letting off the entire cylinder of six bullets at the stykes. They squealed horribly as blood spattered my face.

'Sorry, Grandma. Sorry, Crazy Wolf,' I apologised as they wiped styke goop off themselves too. When I looked back over the ledge I saw that Jez had gone.

'She's gone for some good rope, can ya hang on?' the mayor called.

'Hope so,' I shouted back. The rest of the stykes, on seeing the carnage, had retreated back into the gloom for now but I was sure they'd be back.

Luckily though, Jez was soon rushing up to the bottom of the ledge with a rope, tossing one end up to me. I caught it first time, securing it to an outcrop of jagged rock. Crazy Wolf climbed over the ridge first then waited near the top to help Grandma down. I held the rope steady as they both descended slowly.

When they were safely on the ground, I clambered to join them.

Jez came over and hugged me—no sign of our fall out over the pendant the other day—before hugging Yenene and my uncle. 'Y'all are the last folk I figured I'd see down here—can't hardly believe my own eyes. But how'd ya get here an' what's this 'bout a big vent?'

I gasped, hardly able to get the words out quick enough—there was so much to catch her up on. 'Jez, remember that troll you told me was real mad with the High Sheriff and had been organising all the protests and stuff?'

'Yeah, Sixsnakes, weren't it?'

'Jake Sixsnakes. Yes. Well, he's the reason we're here.'

'What? You kiddin' me?'

'I wish I was. And Jake ain't a troll, he's a rock demon. Can do magic too, dark magic. He's raising an army among the mid-rock trolls to overthrow the sky cavalry and set himself up as ruler of the West Rock.'

'Overthrow the sky cavalry? Even a demon ain't gotta chance o' doing that.'

'I know the sky cavalry are strong, Jez, but so is Jake, and with dark magic on his side he's a real force to be reckoned with. Got close seventy years ago when he first rode out terrorising the rock. He killed my great-grandpa and grandma, and probably would have succeeded in taking over the whole rock only Yenene bound him and tossed him into a well.'

Jez gasped, staring at Yenene. 'You mean he's been down there all that time?'

Grandma nodded. 'Up till the collapse of the western arm released him from his rocky prison, giving him the chance to terrorise the West Rock all over again.'

190

'I know this Sixsnakes,' said the mayor. 'Like no troll I ever seen. He was here a while back. He approached me for my support in the revolt against the sky cavalry but I said I wanted none of it. He was pretty mad.'

'This might sound crazy,' I said, 'but if I didn't know better I'd swear he had somethin' to do with the landslide that trapped all the Deadrock folk here.'

'Me too,' Crazy Wolf agreed.

'But how does all this link up with you arriving in Deadrock?' Jez asked.

'Jake's stronghold is in a place called Stoneforest, a town on the edge of mid-rock that's full of natural holes. He kidnapped Grandma and took her there, so we rode out after him—confronting him inside this huge stone pillar he lives in. He was going to kill us but we escaped by leaping into a hole. We must have fallen halfway down the length of the West Rock.'

Crazy Wolf cupped his hands adding, 'A little wind-ball magic helped us survive with a few cuts and grazes.'

'Some good news is there might be a way out for the folks of Deadrock up the hole we discovered, but cos it's in Stoneforest means we gotta deal with Jake first.'

Jez frowned. 'Why'd Jake kidnap Yenene?'

'He was looking for the scorpion pendant . . . That pendant was the secret to restoring his powers again, not to mention his body.'

Jez looked at Yenene. 'That's why you were acting kinda weird 'bout me having it?'

'Feel bad about it, Jez, but least now you can see I wasn't going crazy.'

The mayor sighed. 'You folks have been through the mill—y'all are welcome to stay at my place till they unblock the tunnel.'

'Thank you, Mayor, but I gotta get word to the High Sheriff about Jake urgently. Jez you reckon I could crawl out the vent with you?'

'It's very narrow but ya ain't put that much beef on ya for being a year older.' Jez grinned. 'Reckon you should just about squeeze through. I was planning on leaving in the morning anyways to update the other soldiers and see if they want me to do another supply run.'

'Good idea, but you are all, I'm sure, very tired,' said the mayor. 'Get some shut-eye, start out tomorrow.'

I didn't want to hang around Deadrock any longer than I had to but every bone in my body ached from our journey through the caverns and tunnels of the mid-rock and I was exhausted. My day had started at Crazy Wolf's tepee and now ended here. 'OK, then, we'll go first thing in the morning.'

The mayor led us through the streets of Deadrock, stopping outside an empty shop window.

I was amazed to see the dwarf baker—looking a whole lot thinner than when I'd last seen him—sitting outside his store. When I'd been in Deadrock last year hunting Pa's killer I'd bought some bread off him. I wondered if he'd recognise me, but it had been a long time and he didn't much look like he cared about anything right now except getting something to eat.

'You there, Baker. There's a whole bunch o' styke carcasses back at the big ridge on the edge o' town, can you fetch 'em an' cook 'em?'

'Aye, be glad to, Mayor.'

'And make sure the kids get some. There are children who haven't eaten properly for weeks.'

'Sure thing.'

We walked on and he turned to us with a grin. 'Realise they coulda killed ya but you did us a favour luring them stykes outta the belly o' the rock; big juicy ones too. They been keepin' their distance of late; folk in this here city are desperate, and it's like they can sense it. For a while it used to be the stykes preyed on us, now it's us preying on them.'

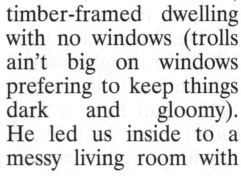

The mayor's house was an end, timber-framed dwelling with no windows (trolls ain't big on windows prefering to keep things dark and gloomy). He led us inside to a messy living room with

194

just a few chairs—Jez and I sat on the floor—and a saddlewood lamp. The living room opened onto a small kitchen towards the back of the house, containing a long wooden table, on top of which was a white tablecloth and an empty fruit bowl.

'What more in the way of supplies do you have?' I enquired.

The mayor looked solemn. 'Much o' the food we have left is going bad. Some are still eating it, though, and it's makin' 'em sick.' He carried a bowl from the kitchen and set it in front of Yenene. 'The stykes you led to us will be cooked and fed to the children and sick but I have a little dried beef, ma'am. You look like you could use it.'

But Yenene put up her hand, stubborn as ever. 'Give my portion to the children too, Mayor. I'm not hungry.'

I was quite taken aback by the mayor's hospitality. He was a rattlethroat troll, so he had no belly snakes, just a voice more gravely than a barrow full of mine ore, and I didn't know them for their friendliness to elves. Then I remembered Pa saying that rattlers were more civilised than snake- bellies.

I spoke to the mayor. 'You might not recognise Jake now—he's got flesh. The pendant I mentioned has worked a magic, restoring him to how he was before he was bound and cast into a well.'

The mayor spat a gobbet of saliva. 'I despise demons even more than mine wraiths. So he's lookin' for support among the mid-rock troll leaders, is he? Pretty worrying. Havin' skin on them bones might win him more support as they'll see him as one of them now. Hate to say it but trolls can be fickle critters.'

Another saliva gobbet was jettisoned from his thick warty lips. 'Bout this hole y'all came from then, ya reckon there might be a way out for the people of Deadrock?'

'Yeah,' I said. 'It's real deep but if there's one thing there's no shortage of on the rock it's good strong rope.'

'And what about Jake Sixsnakes? Can't imagine he's just gonna let the sky cavalry ride into his town and start telling him what to do.'

'The High Sheriff is a good man. He's helped me a lot in the past—I trust him to know what to do.'

'So you'll follow young Jez outta here in the morning.' He smiled at her. 'She's been a big help. She's made more than a few trips back and forth through the vent, bringing vital supplies and risking her life from dust-rat attacks.'

'All part of my duties, sir. I was glad my experience in the vents was able to help you folks.'

I looked at Grandma. 'Will you and Uncle Crazy Wolf be OK till we come back?'

'Have to be,' Grandma shrugged. 'We ain't got much choice.'

Crazy Wolf nudged her. 'We'll be fine, Will. The Great Spirit will keep both us and the mayor here safe until such time as we all get out.'

'Got plenty o' room, and you're welcome to stay till we *do* find a way out,' said the mayor.

I didn't like leaving them down

here but I couldn't see we had too many options right now and the mayor seemed like quite a civilised critter by Deadrock standards. I figured they'd be safe with him.

So we made our plans to leave Deadrock by the air vent first thing tomorrow. We'd travel to Fort Mordecai to warn the High Sheriff about Jake Sixsnakes while telling him too of the potential escape hole for the folk of Deadrock.

Chapter Ten

★

The Crawl to Fort Mordecai

I woke the next morning—at least I figured it was morning—to Jez humming to herself as she packed a bag at the kitchen table.

I stretched and yawned, and she glanced over; 'Good mornin', Will. I thought we'd make an early start.'

She had still been up talking to the mayor when I'd gone to bed and I asked, 'Don't you ever sleep, Jez?'

She laughed. 'A little. Sorry, Will, but there's no breakfast.' She handed me a glass of water.

'That's OK. We can eat when we get to the outside, these folks can't, I don't wanna take anything from them.'

'What's in the bag?'

'Water and stuff for the crawl, and a note from the mayor with an update on the situation here.'

'I can carry something.'

'You'll barely squeeze through

yourself without carrying stuff too—I can manage.'

'Seems kinda weird leaving Grandma and Crazy Wolf in the care of a troll, even if he is the mayor.'

'They'll be fine, the mayor's actually OK. I've gotten to know him pretty well over the time I been here. In fact, it's a different town now—even the troll outlaws are too hungry to cause trouble brawling and shooting.'

I could hear Grandma snoring like a piglet upstairs. I figured there was no point in waking her and my uncle. They knew where we were off to, and now it was up to us to get to the High Sheriff and tell him about Jake's evil plan to take over the West Rock.

I scribbled a note and left it on the table. It read:

Sooner we get going, sooner we get you all out. Sit tight and take care.

Will & Jez

Deadrock couldn't have been any deader, I decided as we walked through town. This was a whole different place than when I'd last visited. I realised it was early but I'd figured there'd be at least a few signs of life. Like Jez said, maybe everyone was too hungry and had no energy to be up and about.

Even the buildings looked hungry: tall skinny wooden buildings squashed together like organ pipes.

Last time I'd been here, I remembered there'd always been the smell of food cooking, baking bread and sizzling sausages. Now there was no such smell. Just damp and mustiness; the smell of a stagnant city—a city that hadn't had any fresh air blow in from the entrance tunnel for weeks.

We passed the empty saloon, purple saddlewood light spilling onto the cobbled street. Then we headed along the track that weaved a precarious route out of town through stalagmites and uneven ground, past the freight station, its platform strewn with barrels and food containers—all empty—on to the tin mine.

A couple of small saddlewood lamps hung at the entrance and, taking one down, we started out into the mine, keeping to the narrow gauge track that ran along the middle of the tunnel.

After a while Jez pointed to a vent. 'Here it is. This hole is our ticket outta here. Y'all set?' She opened her bag and tossed me a pair of gloves, pulling on some herself.

'Cavalry issue,' she informed me. Next she grabbed what looked like some old bits of rag. 'Wrap these round your knees.'

Jez took off my hat, flattened it and shoved it in her bag, then she climbed onto the ledge halfway up the mine wall and disappeared into the vent. I followed.

It was narrow—really narrow, and I decided I'd either grown a bit or it was a different vent to the ones I'd crawled in over a year ago. Either way I was dreading every centimetre. We made slow progress. The only noises were our breathing and our hands and knees shuffling over the rock.

As we crawled, time seemed to melt away, like there was no room for it. And it wasn't long before fear crept up alongside me like a big hairy coach spider. What if there was another landslide? What if the vent caved in? Would Yenene and Crazy Wolf be OK in the troll-mayor's house? Was Moonshine safe up in Stoneforest?

I was glad when the passage widened enough for us to sit down and rest, not to mention have a much-needed drink from Jez's water bottle.

After a long swig, Jez said, 'Still can't believe all the time that little scorpion pendant was magic *and* that it had demon's blood inside it—yuk!'

I took some water then wiped my mouth. 'There's no reckoning what he's capable of now he's up to full strength and got the troll leaders onside. The sooner we get outta this vent and up to Fort Mordecai to tell the High Sheriff about Jake's plan to take over the rock the better!'

'We can stop him. We've proven to

be a good team before and we'll do it again.'

Suddenly I heard something shuffling over the rock up ahead, travelling towards us. I felt my heartbeat quicken. 'I think we got company.'

Jez unsheathed her bone-handled knife from her belt as the shuffling got closer. 'Think you're right.'

The noise echoed in the narrow passageway, and moments later teeth flashed in the lamp light—dust-rat teeth! With an ear-piercing squeak, the brown-coated critter emerged slowly from the gloom then stopped. Jez positioned herself on her knees and sat, rock-still, as the huge rat gawked at her with its beady black eyes. Then with another shriek, the rodent launched itself wildly at her throat. But in a lightning-fast move Jez brought her fist—which gripped the knife—to her throat, and the rat impaled itself on the dagger-sharp blade, its blood spattering Jez's face.

Lowering the knife, she removed it from the dead animal.

I shuddered. 'You OK?'

'Yeah, thanks.'

'Sure got him good.'

'I got that one but there might be more, we'll have to crawl carefully and keep an ear out for 'em.'

We allowed ourselves a short while longer, then, after another drink, set off once more. I hoped there'd be no more rats—or any other obstacles to us getting out. There was no time to waste—Jake was more than likely rallying his evil army to ride to Fort Mordecai and battle.

Finally I saw a glimmer of light up ahead and my heart leaped.

Jez cried, 'We're out!'

'Not a minute too soon,' I gasped. 'Reckon my knees are ready to explode. Being in there was even worse than I remembered.'

Jez crawled out of the vent first then I emerged, blinking, to crawl onto a ridge on the side of the West Rock. I stole a look over the edge and saw it was a sheer drop into the Wastelands. I didn't want to put a foot wrong out here.

We made our way carefully down a narrow track to where the ridge widened. A voice called, 'Howdy, Jez! Weren't expecting you so soon. I'm still getting your next supply run ready.'

A young sky-cavalry soldier was unpacking some wooden boxes filled with packs of what looked like the dried beef strips the mayor of Deadrock had offered Yenene last night.

'Howdy, Clay. But I ain't goin' back in there. I'm going to Fort Mordecai—important news to pass on.'

Spotting me stumble down the ridge after Jez (she'd had a lot more practice at negotiating the precarious rock side than me), Clay made a grab for his rifle.

'It's OK,' Jez grinned. 'This here's Will Gallows, a good friend o' mine. He's the reason I ain't goin' back to Deadrock—for now, anyways.'

'Pleased to meet you, Clay.' I shook his hand. 'We got important information for the High Sheriff. An evil snake-bellied troll rock demon is mustering an army, and plans to ride to Fort Mordecai with the intent of crushing the sky cavalry.'

I told Clay about my encounter with Jake in Bighorn Rock. When I'd finished his cheeks were more than a couple of shades lighter.

'Demons, trolls and a revolt against us—sounds to me like the kinda info the High Sheriff should know immediately. I totally agree you should both head for the fort without delay.'

'We plan to,' said Jez, 'but we need a ride.'

He pointed down the ridge to where a shiny black windhorse stood nibbling some tangleweed. 'You can take Koal, he's a good strong cavalry horse.' Then, with a grin, he added, 'Just don't forget about me down here.'

I smiled. 'Thanks, and don't worry, as soon as we get to the fort we'll make sure to have Koal flown back to you again.'

Starting down the ridge with us, Clay asked, 'How are the folk in Deadrock holding out?'

'Barely,' said Jez. 'They're all starving. The beef strips and medical supplies are helping a bit but I'm only scratching the surface—we really need to get them outta there before it's too late. Any news of the excavation in the Deadrock tunnel?'

'Yeah, it's going slower than an old snail,' Clay sighed. 'We're still waiting for a chance to break through but the tunnel is just too unstable.'

'There might be another way out but it's in Stoneforest—Jake's hangout—so we need to deal with him first.'

Clay gasped, 'A way out up on the mid-rock? You're kiddin' me?'

I shook my head. 'No sir.'

'Will discovered a hole that runs all the way from Stoneforest to a cavern near Deadrock,' Jez informed him.

'Wow! How'd you come by it?'

'I fell into it, well jumped, actually, trying to escape from Jake.'

'Well I'll be, I've heard about them natural holes round that part of the rock but never reckoned on them being that deep.'

The windhorse gave a whinny as we approached and Clay gave him a pat on the neck. I really missed Moonshine right then.

'Well, he's all yours, and you can be sure he'll get you to the fort quicker than the Mid-Rock Flyer itself at full steam.'

'Don't worry, we'll take good care of him. I own a windhorse too, name

of Moonshine—she's stranded in Stoneforest, probably wondering where I got to.'

'Thanks, Clay,' Jez added. 'Catch up with you sometime soon.'

We mounted Koal, Jez behind me, and took to the sky, flying upwards away from the ridge.

'Your horse, Moonshine—pale white mare, ain't she?' Koal critter-chattered as we flew.

'That's right, you know her?'

'I remember you all from the battle near Gung-Choux Village, must be some months ago now. Moonshine was pretty brave in a fight, I'll say that. Had all the makings of a good sky-cavalry horse.'

I grinned. Shy would'a been pleased to hear that. I made a note to tell her when I saw her again.

I told Jez what Koal had said and she laughed too. 'She'd just love that.'

'Her pa was a sky-cavalry horse and she reckons it's in the blood. Sure am worried 'bout her, though.'

I felt Koal shudder through the saddle. 'I overheard you mention

Stoneforest before, she ain't really there, is she?'

'That's where I last saw her.'

'Don't seem like a place a horse would wanna hang around. We cavalry horses are trained to make our way back to the fort when we're separated from our rider. Moonshine got some cavalry blood in her, maybe she flew on home.'

'Hope so,' I said. Though I wondered where home was now Jake had torched Phoenix Heights to the ground.

I gave Koal a pat on the neck as I caught sight of the top edge of the mid-rock jutting out into the misty sky, and next thing we were soaring over marshes, inland towards Mid-Rock City. He was a great windhorse—not as good as Moonshine, though, obviously.

Landing on the outskirts of town, we rode straight to the fort in grim silence and discovered that there were no protesters, and even better the gate was now open again.

'It's daylight—too bright for the troll protesters,' I observed.

Jez smiled. 'Great, I hated having to battle my way through them.'

The sentry, hardened by all the trouble over the past weeks, glared and barred the way with his rifle when he saw me but reluctantly stepped aside at the sight of Jez wearing her cavalry uniform.

Inside, we dismounted and Jez led the way along a row of one-storey wooden buildings past a group of soldiers, busily cleaning both of the fort's stone-spitters. Stone-spitters are probably the most destructive weapon on the whole of the rock—more powerful than the fiercest tornado.

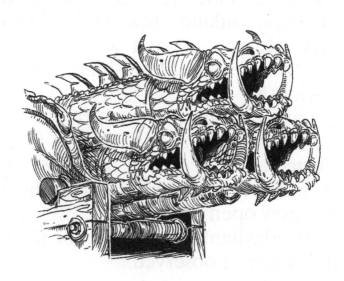

They consisted of long, cylindrical barrels of iron fixed in a triangular shape to a sturdy wooden base (one had three barrels, the other had six). Each barrel end was wrought into the head of a fearsome, open-mouthed thunder dragon. They were chillingly detailed, even down to the dagger-sharp lower canines and cold staring eyes. A pile of rounded boulders known as sky rocks sat piled beside them—they'd be fired with devastating results.

'I wouldn't have to think twice 'bout firing one of them boulders at Jake,' I commented to Jez as we passed.

As we neared the High Sheriff's office a dark-haired soldier hurried over. 'Say, you two wouldn't happen to know anything about a white windhorse we picked up hanging about the outside of the fort now, would ya?'

Jez and I both looked at each other. 'Moonshine!' I gasped. 'Yes, she's mine. Where is she?'

'Stable, we gave her something to eat

and drink.'

'Thanks.' I knew where I was headed before seeing the High Sheriff!

Moonshine whinnied loudly as we entered the stable.

'Will, I was really starting to worry. Last time I saw you, you were going inside Bighorn Rock to find Jake. Where ya been?'

'Long story, Shy, I'll fill you in later. But we found Yenene and she's OK—she's with Crazy Wolf in Deadrock.'

Moonshine's eyes almost popped out of her head. *'Deadrock?!'*

'Like I say, it's a long story and there ain't time to tell it now, we're going to see the High Sheriff. You have any problems lying low in Stoneforest?'

'Had my moments. I ran into that gang of goblins from the Panting Wolf saloon again, but I got away—gave one a kick on the head he won't forget for a while. I decided you'd head here at some point, so came this way.'

'Ya done like a good cavalry horse should comin' here,' Jez beamed, giving Shy a pat on the neck.

'We'll catch up later, Shy, I promise,

214

but right now we gotta go see the High Sheriff.'

'What about Jake, did you find him?'

'Later, Shy,' I insisted. 'Get some rest—you been through it making your way here from that spirit-forsaken place.'

Before leaving the stable I instructed one of the hands to return Koal to Clay, on the ridge near Deadrock. Then we walked back to the corner of the fort, to the High Sheriff's office, where I knocked on the door.

'Come!' a voice boomed.

The High Sherrif stood up from his desk as we entered. He was tall with a kind face, pale blue eyes, white hair and moustache, and wore a knee-length coat.

'Jez, you're back!' the High Sheriff beamed. 'And, Will Gallows, good to see you again, son.'

'You too, sir,' I said. I'd gotten to know the High Sheriff pretty well and figured him to be a just man (my pa did too when he was alive). Like Jez, the High Sheriff once told me I should consider joining the sky cavalry, and

coming from him that was a pretty big deal.

'You had breakfast yet?'

We shook our heads and he opened the door hollering in the direction of the kitchen for a cook to rustle up some eggs and fried bread for three and that we'd be over shortly.

'I made several trips to Deadrock with supplies, all with success,' Jez informed him. 'But while I was there,

216

Will came staggerin' from a hole in the rock with serious news.'

I informed the High Sheriff of all the terrible happenings of the last few days—the ranch fire and Grandma's kidnapping, the pendant, meeting Jake in Stoneforest and learning of his plot to destroy the sky cavalry . . . Finally, I told him the less gloomy news of a possible way out for the starving folk of Deadrock via the hole in Bighorn Rock—but that all hinged on getting rid of Jake. He listened attentively, blue eyes widening more and more as I spoke.

'Of course I know of this lowlife, Sixsnakes—he's the one been organising all the protests of late and there are even some old records in the fort archives about all that mayhem on the West Rock many years ago,' said the High Sheriff, his forehead furrowing. 'And you say he is a demon in the guise of a snake-bellied troll?'

I nodded, 'A killer who has the power to wield deadly dark magic.'

'Wraiths, demons, evil critters, well I got a big crate o' Wynchester Demon

Shots—we'll snuff out that treacherous demon's soul for good. Let his troll supporters see him for what he really is—nothin' but an evil spirit. Trolls got no love for wraiths, so the key might be to expose Jake as nothing more than a jumped-up ghost.'

'Key is also getting into Stoneforest—whole place is like a troll fortress with lookouts posted at the entrance.'

The High Sheriff unlocked a door at the back of his office then turned round.

'Follow me. I want to show you something.'

Jez and I followed him into another room, dominated by a large table. On it was a scale model of part of the mid-rock . . . A part I'd got to know quite well over the past days.

I gasped. 'Stoneforest.'

The High Sheriff nodded. 'We've been keeping an eye on this evil town for a long time—like Deadrock it's worth the watching.'

I pointed to the column of rock with its distinctive jagged peaks near the

back of the town. 'There's Bighorn Rock, that's Sixsnakes' place, and that smaller rock tower up top is where the hole leading to Deadrock is!'

The High Sheriff stroked his chin, nodding. 'The trolls of Stoneforest think they've created a "no go" area for the sky cavalry, well, they're gonna have to think again. I've been waiting for the right time to ride in and sort things out in that town, and your news, Will, has made up my mind that the right time is now!'

'But what about the lookouts— they'll spot cavalry horses a mile away—unless . . .'

The High Sheriff looked at me. 'Unless what?'

'It's nothing, it's a little crazy . . .'

'Spit it out, boy, and though you ain't a soldier . . . yet, that's an order.'

Jez nudged me, 'Yeah *yet*, ya hear him, Will Gallows?'

I grinned, suddenly wondering if maybe my idea wasn't that crazy really. 'Well, what if we don't use horses?'

One of the High Sheriff's bushy grey eyebrows crawled quizzically up his forehead like a caterpillar. 'No horses? But we're the sky cavalry.'

'What if we approach via this lake at the rear of the town?' I tapped my finger on quite a large area behind Bighorn Rock that was coloured blue. 'They'll easily spot horses . . . but I reckon there's less chance o' them spotting boats!'

'Boats!' The High Sheriff slapped his thigh. 'It's brilliant, Will! Crazy but brilliant! We'll get to organising it right away—and spend today getting the boats into position. I don't plan on hanging around any longer than I have to, we're gonna sort out this demon Sixsnakes critter once and for all.'

Chapter Eleven

★

Terror in the Gorge

The High Sheriff meant what he said about not hanging around, and the next day about noon—when all the Mid-Rock City trolls would be asleep—Jez and I rode out with a large troop of cavalrymen, led by the High Sheriff himself, headed for Stoneforest.

We left by the fort's rear exit just to be doubly sure we wouldn't be seen—who knew if Jake had lookout men up here?

'Can't believe it only took the fellas yesterday afternoon to get all the boats transported by cart over to the lake behind Stoneforest,' Jez commented as we rode out. 'Was a real good idea of yours, Will.'

Jez and I rode near the back. Moonshine held her head high, proud to be riding alongside real sky-cavalry horses. I glanced admiringly at Jez who wore a new uniform—the knees

222

had holed through in her old trousers with all the crawling. I was starting to get used to her being a soldier now—she sure looked the part. I glanced down at my own shabby clothes, still the worse for wear from the vent, and for a second tried to imagine how I'd look in a sky-cavalry uniform. I heaved a sigh. I kinda stood out when part of me longed to fit in. It seemed to always be like this. Where did I fit? As a sky cowboy on a cattle ranch, as a mage in Gung-Choux Village or as a soldier in Fort Mordecai?

Once we were out into open country, the High Sheriff gave the order and we took to the air. I spurred Moonshine onto full gallop and she spread her powerful wings, lifting me into the air to soar over the scorched landscape.

Just as the High Sheriff had shown me on the map, we flew in open sky off the edge of the mid-rock, following a westward course round the back of the Edge Mountains then inland through a steep valley. I could just make out the tall dark pillars and peaks reaching high into the sky. Stoneforest looked as ominous and forbidding from the back as it did from the front—though it was more spaced out, with lots of trees and grass, and, of course, the lake. I spotted Bighorn Rock in the distance, its distinctive stone horns jutting into the dull sky.

While we were still a good distance from the troll town, the High Sheriff gave the order to land and we galloped overground the rest of the way. 'High Sheriff says the key element in this whole operation is to take the rebel trolls and Jake Sixsnakes by surprise,' I told Shy.

The land was mostly barren and wild; coarse long grass and a few clumps of trees—there were no farms or railroads here. A chill wind chased down from the hills, blowing along stagecoach-sized balls of tumbleweed. More than a few times, Moonshine had to swerve to avoid being hit, and I was glad she was so nimble; I was sure if you were struck by one it would bowl you off your feet.

As we drew close to the rear of Stoneforest, the High Sheriff consulted a map he had of the town and rode off up front scouting out the landscape. We journeyed through a small patch of woodland, emerging at the beautiful lake of shimmering blue water.

And there tied up on the banks of the lake were five boats that a detachment of soldiers had transported into position yesterday. Each was capable of taking maybe ten men.

'Cool,' said Jez as we dismounted. 'Ain't ever been in a boat. Have you, Will?'

'Fishing in Gung river with my pa and uncle, but these boats are bigger.'

'Not sure if dwarf legs make good sea legs.'

The High Sheriff strode alongside us grinning. 'You're gonna find out, Jez, unless you wanna swim to Bighorn Rock!'

'Can't swim, sir. Had no call to learn. Rivers in the Wastelands, where I grew up, are 'bout as rare as a handsome troll.'

The High Sheriff called for the troops to untie and make ready the boats. 'These craft will take us the short boat trip into the back of Stoneforest and quite near to Bighorn Rock where Will tells us Jake is resident. Keep your eyes and ears peeled, and weapons at the ready. Although the town is guarded mainly from the front, I can't rule out whether Jake has posted trolls along this route, so proceed with caution.'

I turned to Moonshine. 'Wait here, Shy. We'll come and get you when it's all over.'

'Sure you don't want me to come with ya? I can swim, y'know, maybe I could—'

Part of me wanted her to come along. 'It's too far, Shy, but thanks.'

Suddenly I had a thought and, rummaging in the bottom of Moonshine's saddle bag, I found a little pouch decorated with colourful beadwork. I smiled. 'Ah! I thought I had some.'

'Some what?' asked Jez giving Moonshine a farewell pat on the neck.

'Magic leaves. Just in case. Now all I gotta do is remember how to use them.'

Jez and I boarded the front boat and off we went.

The boats moved quietly along the river, the only sound from the rhythmic swish of the wooden oars as they beat the water. The gorge was really creepy. Shadows crept up the high walls on either side of us. There were fearsome animal drawings: pick-tooth wolves, bears, moon coyotes—and, I suddenly noticed, dark-magic symbols, like the ones in Jake's cavern. Even though I'd seen them before they still sent a shiver down my spine—could we really stop Jake?

Then the silence was broken by the shout of a lone troll gunman, and the gorge echoed with the crack of rifle fire. A soldier beside me returned fire and the troll fell forward from a high-up cave, hitting the water with a splash then sinking. Quickly my eyes raked the rocky sides for more lookouts but I couldn't see any.

We sailed on. Everybody more on edge.

Another noise. Loud and clanking and coming from behind us. I spun round as suddenly a great skull-topped iron gate appeared from a crevice in the gorge and began to judder slowly across the water to the other side creating a barrier. Trolls were skilful with mechanical stuff—skills learned through years of rock excavation, mining and rail engineering. Pa used to say that most trolls had the brawn for such work but far fewer had the brains.

'What's happening?' Jez cried.

'We must've sailed through some kind of trip mechanism,' I gasped, 'and activated the gate.'

'It's blocking our escape.'

Did Jake know we were coming? Maybe our idea of surprising him had failed already?

'Looks like Jake's not taking any chances—I'm pretty sure he's set this up to ward off intruders,' said the High Sheriff. 'Keep rowing, and faster!'

As he spoke, there was another low, grating rumble, and the water rippled, the boats lurching in the water.

Jez stared at me wide-eyed. 'Don't like the sound of that.'

Suddenly the gorge wall jerked, and little pieces of rock broke off from the sides to tumble into the lake like drops of stone rain. Rock quake? No! Too mechanical. This was something else. There were clanking metal noises, like some huge machinery hidden deep within the rock, and then to my horror, the gorge walls began to move. Slowly, both sides of the cavern began to come together, squeezing the river into a narrower and narrower channel of

water.

'The whole darn, spirit-forsaken place is closing in on us,' the High Sheriff called.

But there was worse to come. Up ahead another iron gate appeared and began to close over, blocking that way too.

'What are we gonna do, Will?' screamed Jez.

The High Sheriff was screaming orders at his soldiers who unleashed a volley of shots at the gate—but in vain, the bullets doing nothing to stop its progress.

I had a thought. Taking off my shirt and boots and hat I moved to the edge of the boat.

'Will, what you doing?'

I turned to the High Sheriff. 'I say we go under, see what mechanism's driving the gate then try to stop it somehow. Who's with me?'

'Have you gone crazy? It's way too deep, you'll drown!' cried Jez.

'Chance I gotta take.' I had to do everything I could to stop Jake—he had murdered my grandma's family.

'All I know is if this gorge comes together, I won't have to worry about not being skinny enough to follow you through the vents.'

'I'm with you, Will,' said Ford, one of the soldiers. 'Good idea! Mort, you're a strong swimmer, comin'?'

Mort tore off his shirt with a grin. 'Heck, why not—if nothin' it'll cool me off.'

'Great!' I called to the High Sheriff. 'I'll be right back, sir.' Then I dived headfirst into the water.

It was freezing cold. Swimming over to the gate, I took a big lungful of air then dived to the bottom of the lake. I saw that the base of the gate was fitted with coach-sized wheels that ran along a metal track on the river bed. If we could somehow jam even one of the wheels then it might buy the High Sheriff some time to get the boats through.

My eyes frantically raked the bottom of the river. A clump of boulders lay not far from the gate. I signalled underwater to the other soldiers, pointing desperately at the big

rocks. Using all my weight, struggling to keep my breath in, I somehow managed to dislodge one and carry it over to the gate to thrust it under the wheel. The others, realising my plan, grabbed boulders too—more easily than I had—and swam to place them with mine. Closer and closer the wheel moved towards our rock pile, till with a loud clank it struck the boulders. I had hoped the wheel would've derailed off the track completely and gone into the lake bed but it was too much to wish for. There was hope, though—the gate began to move much slower, impeded by the rocks. I'd bought us some time. My lungs burning, I swam to the surface and took a big gulp of air.

Ford, surfacing alongside me with Mort, spat out a mouthful of water. 'That was some mighty quick thinking down there, young fella.'

Jez hung over the boat side, extending a hand to help me aboard. 'Ya did it, Will! Are ya OK?'

'Yeah, I'm fine.' I was gasping for breath.

'Spirits alive, you did it all right!' The High Sheriff beamed, helping the other soldiers aboard too. 'But what *did* you do?'

'We shoved a few boulders below the wheel, but it won't hold for long so we gotta row like crazy.' I grabbed an oar. Even the High Sheriff took one up and rowed with us.

'Dang it, Will,' he gasped as we rowed. 'But there's a soldier in ya just bursting to get out, and when we make it through all this I hope you'll seriously consider joining us, just like your friend Jez here.'

I smiled, feeling a rush of pride. And I was sure Pa, if he was alive, would have been proud of me too. But I

233

couldn't think about the High Sheriff's offer now—I had a bad feeling we were steering into more trouble up ahead.

We sped round a bend in the river gorge. My spine tingled, not from the chill wind, but from the dark-magic symbols painted on the rock walls that were now becoming more and more frequent.

The lake widened and I saw a large grassy expanse, dotted with the occasional large boulder and clumps of trees. Then, behind the trees, a few spaced-out rock pillars, like thick, dark stone totems that towered into the sky, casting long shadows over the ground.

This place was eerily deserted. Where was everyone? I knew we were still very much on the outskirts of town, but on the edge of Mid-Rock City you would run into at least some folk. It made me real nervous.

We landed the boats. From here we would proceed on foot to Bighorn Rock to find Jake. This was it.

Jez handed me a six-shot blaster. 'Here, you'll probably need this.'

I tucked it into my belt. 'Thanks.'

Up ahead the rock pillars were taller and denser; it seemed to be the back of the town proper. The High Sheriff gestured to a shadowy corridor, overgrown with spindly trees, the branches of which looked like old men's hands; they grew out horizontally, creating a green canopy over the gorge. I didn't like the look of it—seemed a good place for an ambush.

The High Sheriff ordered half his men to take up position behind the cover of a range of boulders that scattered the landscape, and the other half to advance with him, towards the gorge.

'Prepare your rifles and demon shots,' the High Sheriff instructed. 'But remember our brief—we are not here to destroy the whole town, only to attack Sixsnakes, and to break down the hold he has on the other troll insurgents. Then we must access the hole Will has told us about, a hole that promises freedom for the folk of Deadrock.'

As he spoke, I stared almost mesmerised into the dark gorge. And two red spots of light appeared, blinking in the gloom.

Chapter Twelve

★

Battle

I swallowed hard, like a big rock pillar had lodged in my throat and my heart raced.

'Jake,' I breathed. I placed my hand on the High Sheriff's sleeve and pointed. 'Sir, I think we got company.'

Jake strode out into the open and stood stone still staring round at us. He was dressed as before in his long duster coat. From beneath it I caught sight of a skull-headed belly snake slithering out to hiss loudly at us.

'You have no jurisdiction on this land, Sheriff, so I do believe you're trespassing.'

'Trespassing? Well now I'm pretty sure I'm standing on part of the West Rock, and as I'm *High Sheriff* of the whole of the West Rock, then I reckon I got all the jurisdiction out here.'

Jake laughed. 'I suppose your arrival is not without its advantages.' He glanced around our number, nodding his head as though counting. 'Now let's see, there must be a third of the sky cavalry with you—I'm honoured. You must be terrified of me to bring so many. When I kill you all it will make it even easier to attack your pathetic little excuse for a fort, destroying it and the remaining cavalry for ever, thus making me, Jake Sixsnakes, ruler of the entire West Rock.'

I shuddered.

'You're deluded, Sixsnakes. I'm bringing you in to stand trial for murder, stirring folk to rebellion, kidnapping, arson and cattle rustling.'

Suddenly I noticed the rock demon direct his red-eyed stare at me. 'Well now, look what crawled out of a hole in the ground! It's the boy fisherman. This is quite something. Perhaps you're made of sterner stuff than I gave you credit for.'

I felt my skin crawl as he looked at me, a grin on his face.

'Give it up, Jake,' I yelled, fear and anger welling up inside me as I thought of him killing my great-grandparents, burning my home to the ground then kidnapping Grandma to bundle her into that awful net like an animal. 'You really stupid enough to think you can defeat the sky cavalry?'

He threw back his head and laughed even louder than before. 'I could ask you a similar question . . .'

He paused as from the darkness, a group of trolls appeared. They wore long leather coats and hats and shouldered huge rifles.

'Are you stupid enough to think that you or your precious little sky cavalry can thwart forces of darkness about which you have absolutely no idea?'

The High Sheriff stepped forward. 'We're not the enemy here, trolls. In fact, we're here trying to help your kinfolk—this young cowboy you were determined on killing along with his family has only gone an' discovered an alternative way into Deadrock cavern and maybe a way o' helping rescue all them poor folk that have been trapped for months.'

'Lies. Lies. Lies. You really think we're going to believe a word that comes out of lying sky-cavalry mouths.'

Some of the trolls looked unsettled by the High Sheriff's words, and their expressions seemed to say they'd have liked to hear more. But Jake was having none of it. He began twisting the High Sheriff's words, shouting, 'All of it lies, men. The low-belly scum is clutching at straws now just because we stopped his little surprise attack.'

At this the other trolls began to nod and cock their weapons. Warty faces scowled, belly snakes writhed under shirts, hungry for a fight.

'We planned no such attack,' the High Sheriff protested.

'Then why sneak in the back way?'

'Would your pinnacle guards have let us ride into the city?'

Jake spat a huge gobbet of bacca weed onto the dirt then he grinned. 'Never!'

'We rode in from the back to *avoid* conflict not provoke it.'

'And I say you're lying. You'll make things a whole lot simpler for yourself if you throw down your weapons and surrender, I might even change my mind about destroying your precious Fort Mordecai—though, y'know, I just really like burning things; the smell of the smoke, the lick of the angry flames devouring everything in their path— something powerful about fire, why, it's almost demonic.'

'You won't get within fifty feet of my fort, Sixsnakes—and as for surrendering, y'ain't gotta chance. Lay down your weapons and I'll see to it that you get a fair trial.'

Jake burst out laughing. 'Oh come now, Sheriff, since when did a snake-belly get a fair trial?'

'You're no troll!'

'All right, then, since when did anyone but human folk and maybe the odd elf get a fair trial?'

I wondered, if Jake had possessed a human body all those years ago would he have found some *other* way to turn the different folk of the West Rock against one another? He was relishing the adoration of his motley band of followers.

And the followers—Jake's smelly, dishevelled troll posse—lurched forward: the snakes of the snake-bellies writhing, the throats of the rattlethroats rasping in a tuneless guttural chant that made every hair on the back of my neck stand up. Then the clearing erupted in deafening gunfire. Rifle and pistol ends flashed, smoke spread, blood spattered on clean cavalry uniforms and filthy troll bark cloth.

I fired off a couple of rounds of my six-shot blaster then dived for the cover of a big boulder. I couldn't see Jez—I just had to hope she'd got herself to safety too.

Jake conjured a torrent of searing hot fireballs that tore through the air, setting trees and bushes on fire and engulfing many soldiers.

In a well-trained manoeuvre some of the sky cavalrymen stood cover, while the rest darted back to join the other soldiers behind the shelter of the rocks. The trolls had no such cover, yet seemed invincible to the bullets.

'Thunder-dragon hide! They're wearing thunder-dragon-hide coats—they'll be bullet proof!' I yelled.

The High Sheriff gasped. 'You're right, Will. Aim for their legs, men, we'll have to take the knees from under them. It's the only way to halt the creatures.'

Many of the trolls stopped to reload, and the High Sheriff shouted orders for the cavalry, who were now behind the cover of the rocks too so there was no chance of shooting their own men. The rocks blazed in a barrage of cavalry rifle fire and many trolls fell, cut down as they advanced, clutching their legs.

As I fired a few more shots, a different, more sinister, attack blew in from the valley. I felt it immediately. It was a fearsome form of dark magic.

Jake cried out, 'Come, strangleweed, do your worst!' And he laughed wildly. The dark balls of evil—like black tumbleweed—rolled down the narrow gully between tall pillars of rock towards the cavalry soldiers, engulfing them. Thrashing, black, root-like limbs dragged the men down, first to their knees—screaming in agony—before they were completely sucked into the ball of darkness that began to roll onwards towards the next group of soldiers. Strangleweed was pure, all-consuming evil that left no trace of its victim, no bones to bury—nothing but a void where once a soldier had stood, face frozen in fear. I'd never seen anything like this before. It was utterly terrifying.

The High Sheriff too looked on in horror as his men were snuffed out in front of his eyes.

I had to act fast. I would use magic to defeat magic. But I'd be using elf magic against dark magic—I was going to try and conjure a thunderball, the most powerful spell in all elf magic. And I had to shut out from my mind the fact that my uncle had only showed me once—and that my latest attempts at magic had all failed. This was no time for error. The lives of these soldiers were depending on me.

'Will, what are you doing?' Jez cried. She noticed me coming out from behind the rock and crawled over.

'Will's run out of ideas but Roaring Dragon just might have a spell up his sleeve.'

Her mouth quivered into a fraught grin as I delved into the small pouch I'd taken from Moonshine's saddle earlier. I took out all the magic leaves and crushed them under my fingers hurriedly as I began chanting the spell in the elf tongue. Without even trying, the words came into my head straight away.

'Wampan obe hokan kwikapawa!'

It worked! Gradually the thunderball formed in my palm, growing bigger and bigger. My heart leaped like a startled frog. It grew and grew, cloud-like steam spinning furiously in my palms, blowing off my hat and pinning my ears to my head, whistling like a tornado.

I unleashed the first thunderball I'd ever conjured towards the advancing strangleweed. Crazy Wolf would have been impressed, I thought.

The thunderball—expanding as it went—tore along the ground and collided with the strangleweed ball, sending it crashing across the clearing into the troll posse then back up the gorge. But the thunderball wasn't finished there. It circled the strangleweed like a tornado then carried it skyward along with some of the trolls as with a loud crash of thunder and stabs of lightning it tore apart the dark murky magic. The strangleweed was no more.

The High Sheriff punched the air. 'Great work, Will!' Then he yelled at a group of soldiers who raised their Wynchester Demon Shot rifles and let off a barrage of blinding light, surging from skull-shaped barrel ends, towards Jake, one bolt of energy only narrowly missing his head.

I heard the rock demon curse then slip below the canopy of branches, heading into Stoneforest.

'Jake's getting away!' I reached for my hat.

The High Sheriff waved his men forward. 'Let's get after him.'

Injured trolls still jeered at us between moans and groans as we passed them.

'You'll never capture him,' one troll sneered. 'He's too powerful—he'll kill you all!'

'We'll see about that,' said the High Sheriff.

Up ahead I noticed the distinctive horn-like rock-top on a tall stone column. 'That's it!' I yelled.

'What?' said the High Sheriff, looking in the direction I pointed.

'The back of Bighorn Rock, the hole is inside that bit—Little Bighorn Rock. But where's Jake?'

As we walked closer I caught sight of a black-winged horse climbing into the sky.

'Look! It's Jake, he's flying away.' The scene looked a little strange. Most trolls prefer flightless horses—but then Jake was no ordinary troll.

'No, he's landed on the top of

Bighorn Rock,' said Jez.

She was right. Why, I had no idea. What was up there?

The High Sheriff began yelling more orders at his men. 'The hole and escape route for the folk of Deadrock is *inside* this rock tower. Six of us will enter to check and secure it while the rest of you stay here and keep

an eye on Sixsnakes up there. Don't let him inside.'

'You can only access Little Bighorn Rock via Bighorn Rock,' I explained. 'There's a connecting tunnel that runs from the main cavern, but be careful, there's a troll guard at the entrance and maybe more inside.'

The High Sheriff nodded, and I watched him busily select the troops who would enter the rock. I wanted to be among them, but I wasn't a soldier—not yet, anyway. Then I heard a familiar neigh. Moonshine soared through the gap between the two rock towers, swooping towards us.

'Shy!' I cried. 'Am I ever glad to see you.'

The soldiers moved back to allow her room to land.

'Been gone a long time, so I figured I'd try and find you,' she panted. 'I didn't wanna miss out on the adventure completely. What's been happening?'

'We found Jake, an' there was a shootout. Lost some men, but then we got the upper hand and Jake's on the run.'

Jez hurried over and gave Moonshine a pat on the neck. 'Good to see you, Shy.'

As she spoke, Jake suddenly cried out in a loud thunderous voice from the top of the rock.

He flung his arms aloft to the dark cloudy sky. I didn't recognise the words he chanted, though it sounded like a magic spell. The wind gusted strongly on the rock top and Sixsnakes's hair blew wildly about his face—he was like some demented beast. With an even louder cry he dropped his arms, and a ferocious bolt of lightning streamed from his fingertips to strike Little Bighorn Rock.

A low rumble echoed throughout the whole of Stoneforest, then came a loud splitting sound, as huge cracks appeared, spreading quickly from the top of Little Bighorn Rock downwards.

'What in spirit's name is he doing?' cried the High Sheriff.

A chill shot down my neck like the cracks in the shattering rock. 'I'm pretty sure he's conjuring some kind of dark-magic spell—and it looks like he's directed it at Little Bighorn Rock, the whole thing looks unstable. We gotta get outta here—and quick!'

I mounted Moonshine and called to Jez: 'Give me your hand.'

She ran over and I hauled her into the saddle behind me. Moonshine didn't need to be told what to do and a heartbeat later we were ascending skyward.

We were barely airborne when a huge chunk at the summit of the rock broke away, tumbling to the ground, scattering the soldiers who had, seconds earlier, stood rooted to the ground in sheer terror. There was more gut-wrenching rumbling as the top of the rock began to crumble, showering down on the stricken cavalrymen who hadn't a chance and were crushed instantly by the falling debris. The whole scene was horrific.

'I could try and go back, Will,' Shy cried. 'See if we can rescue somebody.'

'There's no way I can risk flying us back down there, Shy, even with your skills in the air we'd only be struck by a boulder and killed.'

I saw Jake laugh coldly at the devastation from the safety of his lofty lookout and felt the elf magic burning in my trembling hands. I checked myself. This was how dark magic manifested itself—through rage. Uncle Crazy Wolf had often told me that anger and elf magic are like oil and water—they don't mix and can only beat a trail to the dark side. Little Phoenix's hatred of Jake for killing her husband and oppressing the elf folk had consumed her to the point where she was lured into the very pit of dark magic that, like a disease, ate into her soul until she became a mere shadow of her former self.

The cloud of dust cleared and I saw that only the base of Little Bighorn Rock remained, like a tree stump, but Jake wasn't finished and he directed another bolt of energy into the heart of the base. Cracks formed all over it like river tributaries and it began to crumble in on itself. Horrified, I thought of the six soldiers who were still inside and would be crushed. The rock, as it broke, must be pouring into the huge hole my uncle and I had fallen down only days earlier—the only means of escape for Yenene, Uncle Crazy Wolf, the mayor and all the folk of Deadrock!

Tears welled in my eyes, blurring the scene into a misty grey. My heart hammered against my ribcage like a rodeo horse trying to buck its way out of its stall.

Jake had, in one evil moment, destroyed a third of the sky cavalry and effectively sealed the tomb of hundreds of folk who were trapped in Deadrock. He'd just been toying with us earlier. He hadn't been running away as I'd thought, he'd been luring us to our deaths.

I spotted my Wynchester Demon Shot rifle tucked inside Shy's saddle and pulled it out. 'Fly higher, Shy. Take us to the rock top.'

'What about Jake?' Jez cried.

'Somebody's gotta stop him. And with the sky cavalry crushed, that somebody is you, me and Shy. You OK, Shy?'

Moonshine let out a fearless whinny.

'My pa was the bravest horse in the whole of the cavalry; they used to say he came into his own in situations like this—bring it on!'

Chapter Thirteen

★

On Bighorn Rock

Moonshine soared upwards to the top of Stoneforest, sticking close to the side of the rock for cover. I planned to surprise Jake. He probably reckoned we'd been crushed by the collapsing tower along with the sky cavalry. We had to stop him before he rallied the Mid-Rock trolls and marched on Fort Mordecai, intent on wiping out law and order for good, and then setting himself up as the new, evil ruler of the West Rock.

No sooner had we cleared the peak than a bolt of awesome energy swooped towards us, catching Moonshine on the wing. With a loud neigh she tumbled from the sky, landing on the edge of the rock, and Jez fell from the saddle striking her head on the ground, lying motionless. Jake must have known we were coming for him. Somehow I managed to jump

257

clear and roll across the rock top.

Getting to my feet, about to run to my friends, I came face to face with the demon. He grinned at me sinisterly. 'I've got a way with rock, haven't I? Well, I *am* a rock demon.'

'You don't look too concerned you just blocked the only escape route for the Deadrock trolls. You don't care, do you?'

'Cos I blocked them *in there*, that's why. Thinking this was all the cavalry's fault will get every troll on my side for a revolt. By the way, I should be angry with you—there's a lot of my army injured back there. For some quite twisted reason, though, I'm actually grateful to you. You led the sky cavalry here—and with many of them dead or injured, it's going to make it so much easier when I ride to Fort Mordecai.'

'Why, Jake? Why are you doing this?'

'I'm a demon.'

'That's not a reason. You're contaminated by dark magic.'

'I *am* dark magic. Anyway, what do

you know about such things?'

'That it corrupts, eats away at your soul like rust on metal.'

'Aren't you afraid it will corrupt *you*, Will? Maybe it's already started. You can't take your mind off magic, can you? Can't even focus on your ranch chores?'

'You don't know anything about me.' His words made me uncomfortable.

'Oh, but I do. I know more about you than you think. I know you're of the blood line of Little Phoenix. There's a whole lot written in your blood, cowboy. Blood's important, y'know. Blood's everything.'

'I'm different, it's good elf magic I'm learning.'

'Elf magic, dark magic . . . There's no difference. There is no good magic—magic is an extension of the person who wields it. It is your uncle who is good, that is why the magic he wields is good. Your great-grandmother, on the other hand, was a whole lot different.' He began to tut and shake his head.

'No, Little Phoenix was a good person.'

'Now Yenene, your grandmother, *she* should have learned the ways of the mage—she'd have been the best, better than your uncle.' He paused. 'And what of you, Will Gallows? Dare you even think of learning what's inside you, oh dare you?'

'What would you know about what's inside me?'

'Like I say, more than you think.'

The sky rumbled and another fork of lightning jabbed down from the gloomy clouds, a remnant from the thunderball.

'Bad isn't *all* bad, Will,' Jake went on. 'Sometimes bad can be powerful. Just like me. Forget the sky cavalry; they're going to be history soon. Join me and I'll spare your life.'

'*Join you?* What are you talking about? Join you in what?'

'Total rock domination. You intrigue me, Will. The magic is strong in you. I could use you—never had an apprentice before, it might be rather fun.'

Another crash of thunder. 'Never! I'd rather die than join you, Sixsnakes.'

'That can be arranged. Sooner than you think too. Since you're refusing my offer then I have no need to spare you after I'm through with you. Anyway, it'll make life easier having two fewer medicine mages about—your uncle isn't going to be leaving Deadrock, and you're going to be dead.'

Suddenly I felt the ground give way under my feet. It was like the rock had turned to quicksand, no longer able to support me. I was sinking. I staggered, only just managing to keep my balance.

Stone steps magically appeared beneath me, descending in a spiral staircase. I stumbled onto them and fell downwards. Turning, I tried to go back up, only to find the steps above me had begun smoothing into a slope. *What was this magic?* It was like the staircase was insisting I go down. But to what? I stumbled blindly down the steps as one by one they disappeared at my heels. I had to quicken my pace to keep ahead of them and avoid plummeting all the way to the bottom. It grew darker and darker, until I could see nothing. My heart pounded. It had to be Jake doing this, but why? And what sort of dark magic was he using now?

Then I saw a glimmer of dull purple light appear below me. Saddlewood lit the final steps of my descent into a large deserted cavern. I slowed, taking in my surroundings—this looked like the cavern my uncle and I had stood in only a few days ago when we'd watched Jake address the trolls from Mid-Rock City.

The vanishing staircase quickly caught up with me, becoming a smooth granite slide beneath my feet, and I slid on my behind down the last section, tumbling into the middle of the dim cavern.

Getting to my feet, I soon realised the cavern wasn't deserted. In the far corner, lit by a single branch of saddlewood, was a round saloon-type table. Two chairs had been placed at either end and on one, shuffling a deck of cards, sat Jake—already.

Without taking his crimson eyes off the cards he said, 'I take it you know how to play snake poker?'

I edged closer. I was desperate to get

back and check that Jez and Shy were ok, but what choice did I have?

My fear was turning to curiosity. If Jake was going to kill me why hadn't he done it on top of the rock?

In the middle of the table was a coiled snake. During snake poker the creature is trained to enter a mystical trance, gazing round the table of players with huge eyes, probing their minds for weakness, a glimmer of a thought. If the snake detects a bluffer then it strikes, putting that player out of the game.

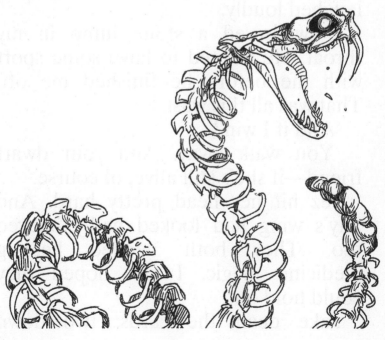

But this was no rune snake, this was a skeleton—one of the belly snakes that poured out of Jake's guts—its pin-sharp canine teeth snapping at the air.

Jake directed a hand to the chair opposite. 'Take a seat.'

'How'd you get down here?' I asked.

'Same way you did.'

I sat as Jake split the pack in two and did an impressive card shuffle on the table in front of me.

'What are we playing for?'

Not raising his fiery stare from the cards he replied, 'Your blood!' and laughed loudly.

I swallowed a stone lump in my throat. He wanted to have some sport with me before he finished me off. That was all this was.

'And if I win?'

'You walk away. And your dwarf friend—if she's still alive, of course.'

Jez hit her head pretty hard. And Shy's wing had looked badly injured too. They both needed healing medicine magic. I just hoped they could hold out.

Jake dealt the cards: two down

then two up. I'd watched the ranch hands play snake poker so I knew the rules. I studied my face-up cards first: seven of bats and a seven of dragons. Not bad. Then, slowly, I thumbed the corners of my face-down cards, raising them a little to take a look: a three of bullets and a queen of dragons. Could have been better. Across the table my opponent had a nine of snakes and a king of snakes showing.

Jake was stoney-faced, his eyes contracting into little pinpricks of glowing red light.

'Can't see how this is a fair game,' I grumbled.

'Why?'

'Cos that ain't a rune snake—it's one o' your belly snakes.'

'Best I could do at short notice, I'm afraid. So for this game it's a rune snake and it'll perform the same task. I'm giving you the advantage. As the snake is a part of me it's got more chance of being able to figure out if I'm bluffing. Another card?'

I discarded my three of bullets, tossing it face down on the table, and Jake dealt me another. A seven of snakes. Suddenly I had three of a kind, a pretty good hand. Not that it probably mattered what I had, Jake's track record for keeping promises stank—I thought of the moment I'd given him the pendant and yet he'd still let go of the net holding Grandma— I'm sure he'd kill me whatever happened here.

I had to think of a plan. I had to think of a way outta this. I couldn't let the card game distract me. Had to think . . .

The snake seemed to sense my torment, and arched its head to start

266

hissing at me.

'You turn up something good there, cowboy?' Jake probed.

I glanced up at him then gasped, recoiling in cold terror. Half of his facial skin had gone, revealing the bloody muscle tissue; parts of his cheek, jaw bone and yellow teeth were now gruesomely visible. This was much worse than when he'd been a skeleton. Blue veins pulsed like tiny writhing worms. I pushed back my seat and retched between my feet.

From his pocket, Jake took out a handkerchief and offered it to me. 'Quite annoying, really—my best poker face and it just falls off my skull. Still, it won't be like this for long—not now I have you here.'

I took the handkerchief and wiped my mouth. 'I don't understand.'

'My blood wasn't the only blood in the pendant.' His voice was chilling. Your great-grandmother, as she prepared the spell with the blood-sucking scorpion, would've known that for the dark magic to be at its most effective she had to add a drop of her own blood. She most likely used the scorpion's sharp limb to pierce her own fingertip, allowing a tiny drop of blood to run down the claw before she encased it in the amber resin with mine.'

'Why are you telling me this?'

'The blood that was in the pendant restored most of me for a while but, as you can see, the magic is waning—the amount of blood in there, though powerful, was a little too meagre to be of any lasting benefit.' His nose dropped off, landing on the table in front of me with a horrid snorting sound. Jake simply brushed it onto the floor. 'I need more.'

My eyes fixed in revulsion on his gaping nose cavity. 'There ain't any more. There was only *one* pendant.'

'But there *was* more than one type of blood in there.'

I stared at him; the back of my neck tingling like a cold snake had slithered under my shirt collar.

Jake went on, an evil grin writhing over his face, 'As you are of the bloodline of Little Phoenix, *your* blood has the power to restore me.'

'My blood? Restore you? But that's

crazy—it don't make sense.'

'Because your great-grandmother's blood was mixed with mine to conjure the spell it means there is a supernatural blood bond between not only myself and Little Phoenix but her descendants too—you, Will.'

'What about Yenene's blood? If you need our family line, why didn't you kill her when you had her?'

'Potential, but I quickly sensed that she was not nearly powerful enough; a result of her complete lack of interest in all things magical. And your uncle Crazy Wolf has too much of his father's side in him. No, it is yours that is just perfect. I thought you'd gone and ruined my plans by jumpin' down that hole. I was worried for a moment. But now you've just walked right back into my hands. Now, stop staring. Call! Come on let's see what you've got.'

I turned over my cards, dumbly. What did it say about me that my blood was perfect for a demon? 'Three of a kind.'

I had barely let go of the cards when Jake's belly snake struck my hand, its dagger-sharp teeth penetrating deep below the skin. The pain was so agonising I cried out.

Instantly, Jake's face began to rebuild. Even such a tiny bit of my blood seemed to be knitting skin over bone, reforming his ugly features.

The snake released me from its pin-sharp grip and I nursed my bleeding hand, tearing Jake's handkerchief to bandage it.

The demon sucked in a lungful of air as he slowly turned over his cards, his cheeks glowing red, warts pulsing on his nose. 'I'm feeling all of a flush,' he gasped. 'A snake flush!' And he laughed uncontrollably.

I suddenly heard footsteps in the cavern and froze. The steps were heavy—was it the sound of trolls approaching?

I groaned as I saw my guess was right. The trolls, who'd met right here in this cavern with Jake while Uncle Crazy Wolf and I watched in secret, entered, shouldering big rifles and dressed for battle.

'Perfect timing, gentlemen. You

arrive just as I defeat my cowboy friend at snake poker. And I see you've come prepared for a much greater defeat—that of the sky cavalry.'

Punk regarded Jake's ruddy complexion with some consternation. 'You look . . . Different.'

'I feel different, Punk. I feel invigorated.' Sixsnakes rose to his feet, and I noticed skin crawl over his knuckles as he flexed his fingers.

'I'd love to play another *hand*,' he said to me. 'But I'm afraid there's no time; I have a rock to conquer. For now you can stay here and enjoy the scenery.'

He strode away, past the stone throne, and suddenly the cavern echoed with an ear-splitting metallic grating noise as steel bars shot down from the roof just beyond the table. I was imprisoned in the corner of the cavern.

'Hey, wait!' I got up and slammed my hands on the bars. 'Let me go!'

'Save your energy, boy. I'm going to need more of your precious blood soon, and I want it to be on top form.'

Punk sneered, 'We've heard news of soldier graves already in Stoneforest. Is it true?'

'A third of the sky cavalry lie under the rubble that was Little Bighorn Rock,' Jake sneered. 'The fort will be ours soon.'

'There are still their stone-spitters to consider.'

'Leave their feeble weapons to me,' said Jake, and then fired a bolt of lightning from his hands which struck the wall sending shards of stone splintering round the cavern. 'Come, the light fades, there isn't a moment to lose. You have horses?'

'Yeah,' said Punk.

'Then let us ride to Fort Mordecai and victory over the sky cavalry.'

Chapter Fourteen

★

Assault on Fort Mordecai

Frantically, feeling my heart pound in my ribcage, I began to rummage around my prison trying to figure a way out. But it was hopeless, the bars were solid iron and I had no more magic leaves to conjure a thunderball.

Then I heard a noise; saw a shadow skulking near the entrance. It looked strangely familiar, small, like a ... dwarf.

'Jez? Over here!' I called. I had never been more pleased to see her.

'Will! Thank goodness. I was mortified I'd find you lying dead somewhere.'

'Rotten demon's keeping me alive, s'why I'm in here. He needs my blood.'

'Your blood?'

'It puts flesh on his evil bones and restores his power somehow. What about Shy? And, you—your head OK?'

'Her wing got a bit cooked but she's

273

OK to fly. She's waiting outside for us. And I'm fine, don't worry 'bout me.'

'Get me outta here, Jez. Jake's on his way to Fort Mordecai—we gotta get there before him and warn them.'

'Sure but . . . how?'

'Look over there by the stone throne, that's where Jake was walking just before the bars came down outta the cavern roof. Maybe he tripped some sort of mechanism.'

Jez hurried over to check round the throne. 'I don't see anything . . . Wait, there's something on the floor here.'

She stooped to examine whatever it was. 'Looks like some kinda lever, maybe if I . . .'

Next thing there was a grating clank as the steel cage juddered then began to rise.

'You did it, Jez! C'mon, let's get outta here.'

There wasn't a troll in sight as we chased outside to find Moonshine waiting nervously in the shadows of the opposite rock tower.

Spotting us, she snorted, flicking her ears. 'Will, you OK?'

'Yeah, what about your wing?'

'A bit singed but I had a test flight down from the top of Bighorn Rock— reckon I'm all right to fly.'

'Good, cos there's no time to waste, we gotta get over to Fort Mordecai and warn the sky cavalry that Jake's on his way to attack the fort.'

Moonshine shuddered. 'Jake sure is a cold-hearted killer— terrible to see so many soldiers lose their lives like that.'

'Ain't nothin' but pure evil, Shy, and he's gone and sealed the tomb of the folk of Deadrock too, with Grandma and Uncle Crazy Wolf still down there.'

Mounting Moonshine, I pulled Jez on to sit behind me again, then we took to the air, flying higher until the tall thin granite towers were like small boulders below us.

We hadn't been going long when Jez

275

cried, 'Look, down there!'

I spotted the ugly lookin' trolls. 'It's Jake's army. Careful, Shy, we don't want them to see us. Jake will be thinking he can take the fort by surprise, but we'll be ready for him.'

'Don't worry,' cried Moonshine. 'I'll take a different route so we don't have to fly over them.'

In spite of her injured wing Shy flew

hard, but she wasn't quite as fast as normal, and I was worried that our detour to avoid being spotted by Jake had wasted too much time. Would we be too late to give the cavalry enough chance to prepare for the assault?

Luckily though it wasn't long till the large central lookout tower of Fort Mordecai came into view.

I gave Moonshine a pat on the neck. 'Good job, Shy.'

We flew towards the rear of the fort. In the corner tower, the lookout guard raised the barrel of his rifle. On seeing Jez's cavalry uniform he lowered it again, signalling for us to fly into the fort grounds. We had no time to lose.

Moonshine swooped in low, over the wooden ramparts, and landed skilfully between the interior fort buildings.

The door of the High Sheriff's office flew open and a worried-looking captain waved us over.

'I fear by your expressions the news may not be good,' he said, herding us inside. 'I've had no message back from the High Sherriff.'

Jez and I told the captain of the

tragic devastation back at Stoneforest, and of the collapse of Bighorn Rock with the loss and injury of many soldiers—including the High Sheriff. He listened attentively, putting a hand to his forehead in dismay. We finished with the bleak report that Jake Sixsnakes and the troll army were fast approaching on horseback.

'This is serious news indeed. How many?'

'Fifty . . . maybe more,' said Jez. 'All heavily armed with six-shot blasters and rifles.'

'Then there's their leader, Jake,' I added. 'He's not a troll, he's a rock demon. He wields dark magic, and his power is incredible, it's like nothing I've seen before.'

'A powerful demon and a troll onslaught, and at the very worst of times—our numbers are badly down. Worse still, there is no time to call on the other West Rock forts for assistance.' The captain frowned. 'This was exactly what this demon wanted, wasn't it? Still, we mustn't waste time dwelling on what we *can't* do. We must prepare for battle. You'll fight with us, Will?'

'Yes, sir. I'd be honoured to.'

'Then make ready the stone-spitters—Private Jez'll show you how—their fire power is unmatchable even against some magic-wielding demon.'

As he'd ordered, we made our way to the stone-spitters, located at the front of the fort where one of the soldiers asked us to help stockpile the rounded boulders that the weapons fired.

We got to work as all around us the fort bustled with frenzied activity. The captain strode up and down barking orders. Cavalry readied themselves and the fort equipment to face the troll onslaught, climbing to the top of the high ramparts, aiming their rifles.

Suddenly the soldier on the guard tower shouted, 'Captain! Captain!' I looked up as, thrusting out the barrel of his rifle, the guard yelled the words we'd been waiting for: 'Trolls, advancing from the east!'

The captain climbed the ladder to the tower two rungs at a time, Jez and I following. At the top, I peered over the flat dusty landscape. Our attackers weren't hard to spot; a great mass of flightless horses, hooves kicking up dust, mounted by burly trolls. I felt my heart quicken. This was it—the battle was on. I wondered what Jake would do when he saw I'd escaped his cavern again.

The light was already beginning to fade, giving the trolls an advantage, and Jake knew it. They moved quickly across the land, and when they were close enough I saw that they were arrayed like a real army in troll battle clothes: black and green hooded cloaks crisscrossed with bullet belts, and carrying triple-barrelled rifles. One troll at the front bore aloft a flag with an image of a coiled snake slithering through the orbits of a skull.

And there, next to the flag bearer, sitting proud in the saddle of a black stallion, sword drawn and urging the troll army forward, rode the evil Jake Sixsnakes.

The trolls numbered more than I'd reckoned on. The demon had sure managed to hoodwink the troll leaders into joining him, with his lies about the sky cavalry not caring about the folk of Deadrock. He had really sold the idea of conquering the West Rock to them. The cavalry were doing their best and this was how they were being repaid—a vicious uprising. The troll army actually believed they could do it. A cold wave of fear crept over me—what if they could? What if the trolls defeated the sky cavalry, what sort of West Rock would it be then? It was hard to imagine. The mayor of Deadrock seemed OK for a rattlethroat troll but I knew there were more snake-bellies than rattlethroats on the rock, and I was pretty sure life under troll authority would be miserable. We had to stop Jake, quell the uprising and restore law and order to the rock.

We climbed back down the tower. Jez scurried off, reappearing moments later carrying two rifles. She tossed me one of them. 'It's great you're gonna fight alongside us, Will. And when this is all over, an' we beat this Sixsnakes demon, you gotta see about joining up for real.'

The troll army halted at the bottom of the hill, close to the fort. I was sure surprised when I saw that a lone rider broke away from the rest of the army and rode up the hill under a banner of truce. The sky-cavalry guards eyed him warily but, honouring the flag of truce, they held their fire.

At the fort entrance the troll handed in a

note to the guard, who brought it up to the captain. He read it aloud: *'I advise you to surrender now or be completely destroyed.'*

Clenching his fists, the captain's face reddened. 'The insolence of Sixsnakes, demanding we just lie down like dogs and let them take Fort Mordecai!'

'Wants us to make it easy for him,' I said.

'Might be a rock demon but he's sure acting like a bone-idle troll,' Jez added.

'Bring me a pen!' bellowed the captain.

The guard hurried back with one, and turning the note over the captain wrote, speaking aloud, *'We will defend the fort to the last man.'* He gave the note to the guard who returned to the fort entrance.

I watched the lone troll rider return to the front ranks of the army and hand the message to Jake. As he read it, Jake's raucous laughter was carried on the breeze up the hill. Then there was an eerie silence as we waited.

We waited for Jake to give the order

to advance. Waited for the thunder of hooves as the great mass of troll-mounted horseflesh advanced. Waited for the loud, ear-piercing crack of rifle fire.

But there came no such sounds.

Only the shrill whistle of a steam train as it cut through the chill evening air. The new Mid-rock Flyer was pulling into the city station. The fort had been built close to it for logistical reasons, in case the cavalry needed to transport heavy equipment to and from the base.

Jez frowned. 'Well that don't look right. Usually the evening train is almost empty, just a few stragglers coming home from a day in the Westwoods. That train's packed!'

The carriage doors opened and folk spilled out onto the platform. Sky cavalrymen, their faces blackened and bloodied, carried troll children in their arms off the train. Others helped adult trolls, skinny, emaciated, some barely able to walk. They headed towards a tall building on the edge of town—Mid-Rock City Hospital—oblivious to what was happening here at the fort.

'It's the folk of Deadrock!' I cried. 'They're free! How have they done it?'

A few cavalrymen from the train made their way towards Fort Mordecai, confusion written on their faces at the sight of the troll army. Confusion that quickly turned to alarm as, suddenly aware of the hostile situation, they reached for their rifles. The captain sent a soldier down from the tower to get word to them about what was happening.

Over where the troll army stood, I noticed the horses stir uneasily as their mounts surveyed the panic, breaking ranks to cluster together in conversation over what was happening.

And then in their midst, I heard Jake scream, 'Attack! Attack!'

The horses neighed loudly as their mounts tried to steer them round to order again, but as they lined up, Punk rode in front of them and held out his hand saying something I couldn't hear. Then he snatched the white banner of truce and rode towards the station.

Spotting Moonshine over near the

stable I called to her. 'Shy, get me down there!'

'No, Will, you mustn't leave the fort, it's too dangerous,' warned the captain, overhearing.

'I don't care, I gotta see if Grandma's down there. I gotta see what's goin' on. I'll report back soon.'

'I'm coming too,' said Jez. 'You'll need a soldier with ya,' she added with a grin.

Hearing the siren of an ambulance, I rode down to the train station where I spotted the mayor of Deadrock alighting from a carriage and hurried over. 'How'd you . . .?'

'The cavalry broke through,' gasped the mayor. 'It's a miracle, they were fearless, spotted a way and just kept digging till they got to us.'

They'd made it! 'And Yenene and Crazy Wolf?'

'Still aboard, but they're both OK. Who are those trolls on horseback?'

'Jake Sixsnakes's army, he's going to attack the fort.' But as I spoke Punk rode up to us, carrying the flag of truce.

'What do you want?' Jez asked.

'The folk of Deadrock are free, then?' Punk enquired.

'Sky cavalry got us out,' the mayor explained. 'No thanks to your leader there, he ain't no friend of trolls—he's a demon imposter. It was him who was responsible for the rock slide that trapped us all . . .'

Suddenly, as if from nowhere, a fire ball struck the mayor on the chest and he fell to the ground.

Jez bent to see he was OK, helping him to one side.

Stunned, I looked up to see that Jake had followed Punk down the hill and now sat scowling on his black stallion, his hands smoking.

'The Wynchester Demon Shot,' I breathed. 'I've left it behind.'

'I'll get it,' said Jez, running off towards the fort.

'Hold yer fire. This is the Mayor of Deadrock, he's done nothing wrong.' Punk stared out Jake. 'This changes everythin', Jake, I'll need to speak to my men. I got family in Deadrock, a brother—I ain't willin' to ride 'gainst

287

soldiers who've toiled bravely to save his life. This ain't the time for battle. There are injured trolls here.'

'This changes nothing,' Jake boomed. 'The sky cavalry are an oppressive force that must be crushed. And this is the best time to attack, when they are weak and confused.'

Punk shook his head. 'No. I'm instructin' my men to withdraw.'

'*Your* men? I am in charge now! They are *my* men! They will do as I say or face the consequences.'

Suddenly Yenene appeared from steps of the nearest train carriage and walked to face Jake. 'Listen to the troll, Jake—it's over. We got no call for a rock demon round here anymore.'

'Grandma!' I shouted. 'Get back!'

Jake stared at her with a hint of disbelief. 'Shouldn't you be at the bottom of a hole?' he sneered. 'And it's over when *I* say it's over. I should have killed you back at Stoneforest. You've got more lives than a rock cat, old woman!'

'Give it up or I'll bind you—for ever this time,' said Yenene

Jake Sixsnakes roared with laughter. 'Bind me with what—your shawl?'

The sky darkened even more, and in the distance great dark twisting balls appeared, moving quickly over the ground.

'More strangleweed! Evil magic that'll destroy everything in its path,' I cried. I wondered if there was a way of warning the cavalry and Jez, but then I saw that it wasn't headed for the fort but those trolls who were still rooted to the spot on Punk's instruction.

'Pathetic, Jake,' said Yenene, staring at the encroaching strangleweed. 'Don't get your way, so you destroy everything. My mother used to say that if you don't believe in ghosts then you won't see one. Well, reckon that could be applied to demons too. Can't you see that folk don't believe in you anymore? No one wants you round here. No one wants you on the rock—and I think it's high time you disappeared!'

'Your parents—whom I killed—were fools,' Jake spat. 'And they raised an even bigger fool. It's time, old hag, that you joined them in the spirit world. Think of it as a kind of reunion of fools.' And he laughed loudly, drawing his sword to thrust it towards her. She stumbled backwards falling to the ground. He moved to stand over her. 'Now this looks familiar, takes me back to when I finished off your ugly witch-faced mother.'

'*Noooooo!!*' I cried.

In the panic, I charged at Jake, striking the sword, flinging it from his grasp. Some of the soldiers fired their rifles too, but the bullets didn't even touch the demon.

A fireball surged past my shoulder to strike Jake in the face. I spun round to see Uncle Crazy Wolf jump off the flyer clutching a lasso, glowing brightly with a steady blue light. He tossed it to Yenene who caught it one-handed.

'Done the magic part, sister, but I'd make a lousy rancher so it's all yours.' He grinned.

Cursing, Jake clutched his face, hair ablaze as I caught an awful whiff of burning flesh and almost retched again. The fireball had disorientated

him but not for long, as he lowered his hands red eyes glowed through scorched flesh; his palms glowed too with expanding fire.

But Yenene, quicker than a wood panther, leaped to her feet and threw the rope, which, like a striking clattersnake, flew through the air, the gaping O of the lasso falling perfectly around Jake's warty head.

Then, pulling the lasso taut, she yelled the binding spell she'd uttered all those years before at the top of her voice.

'Hwan yakan wakipa hakin kaga!'

Jake was caught like a calf in a rodeo, red eyes wide and blinking, his expression drained of colour, mouth twitching. The rope glowed even brighter, a pale blue ghostly light that quickly spread over his body, petrifying him just like that wraith I'd met back at Phoenix Heights all those days ago—even his grotesque belly snakes stopped writhing and froze.

Panting, Jez ran into the station, the Demon Shot slung over her shoulder.

I looked at Grandma. 'You wanna

do this?'

She shook her head. 'Finish him off, Will.'

'Thanks, Jez. Ya sure are a real soldier.' I took the rifle. 'Then this is for Little Phoenix, my great-grandma!'

For the first time I saw a look of fear spread over Jake's scorched face as I strode towards him.

I locked my stare on his demon red eyes.

'You're right about the magic being strong in me, Jake Sixsnakes, but I'm happy to say it's even stronger in this piece of cold steel.'

I pulled the trigger and, with a loud roar that echoed off the city buildings, a lightning-bright beam of magic surged from the barrel ends. The bolt of energy tore into Jake's body, and with a final agonised, demonic cry he began to change for the last time.

The skin that I'd watched crawl over his bones only hours ago now dripped, molten-like, from his frame to once more reveal a pale glowing skeleton that seconds later melted away into nothingness.

And Jake Sixsnakes, the rock demon, was no more.

The strangleweed vanished too, just as it had been about to smash into the troll army.

Moving to where I'd snuffed out Jake's evil soul for good, I noticed something on the ground and stooped to pick it up. The scorpion pendant. Jake had kept it on him. I wondered why. It was bloodless now—what use could it have been to him?

'If it's OK with you, Grandma, I'd like Jez to have this back?'

Yenene nodded, looking for the first time in months much younger than her almost eighty years. 'I'd like you to have it too, Jez,' Yenene agreed. 'I got no need for it now.'

I put the pendant around Jez's neck.

'Will, you sure? I mean it's a family thing.'

Yenene smiled. 'Told you before, Jez, you're the closest thing I got to a granddaughter so in a sense you *are* family.' Crazy Wolf nodded and smiled his own agreement.

I walked over to Moonshine. 'It's

over, Shy. Jake's gone.'

'Wow, sure am glad to see the back o' that rock demon—he creeped me right out!'

'Yeah, creeped me out too, Shy. Let's go home.'

Chapter Fifteen

★

Phoenix from the Ashes

The sign on the desk read:

Behind the desk, a smartly dressed troll rose to his feet, extending a warty hand to shake first Yenene's hand then mine.

'Congratulations on your new ranch, folks,' he said.

'When can we move in?' Yenene asked eagerly.

'Now all the paperwork's finished, don't see why you can't pick up the keys tomorrow. Old Clayton, the previous owner, has long since packed his britches and moved out, so it's all yours.' He placed the documents Grandma had just signed into a drawer. 'Stroke o' luck your old place coming back on the market like that.'

Yenene stood up and pulled her shawl tight around her shoulders. 'Reckon we deserve some luck after what we been through.'

He nodded. 'I know. Terrible business your ranch goin' up in flames like that. Still, I'm sure you'll be happy back here on the eastern arm. You could say ya got yourself a little phoenix from the ashes there, ma'am.'

I caught sight of something wriggle under the troll's shirt, and for a second Jake's ugly face swam before my eyes. It had been almost a month since I'd snuffed out his evil soul for good back in Mid-Rock City, yet those red eyes still haunted my dreams.

The troll was right, we couldn't believe it when we'd spotted our old ranch, Phoenix Rise, up for sale. Even more surprising was that Yenene was so keen on buying it, as it meant moving back to the eastern arm where

I'd be nearer Uncle Crazy Wolf and elf magic. I reckoned Grandma was changing her mind about elf magic—starting to see that it wasn't all bad.

Things had settled down on the rock. The mayor and all the troll folk of Deadrock had quelled what remained of the ill-feeling among the trolls of Mid-Rock City by championing the brave sky cavalry for freeing them from certain death. And there was a new brave member of the sky cavalry—Jez had passed her training and was now a fully fledged officer. Miraculously the High Sheriff and some of the other soldiers who had survived the landslide at Little Bighorn Rock, had escaped with only a few broken bones. Sadly though most of the soldiers who'd fought at Stoneforest lost their lives.

Leaving Rufus Hedd's office—which was a pit house—we walked upstairs and out into the sunlit streets of Dugtown. I squinted. I'd almost forgotten what sunlight looked like it had been so gloomy of late.

'We oughta take a ride by Luke Handold's place and check on our cattle and horses,' said Yenene.

I rolled my eyes at Moonshine who was waiting for us by the water trough. 'I'm sure the cattle and horses are fine, Grandma. They were fine yesterday when we rode by, what could've changed?'

'I know but all the same it's good of Luke to let the steers graze his land till we move in, an' we shouldn't take his kindness for granted. And now we can tell him we got the go ahead to start moving in tomorrow.'

I could tell Grandma was just itching to get back to ranching again. The last weeks she'd been like a cowboy without a horse—moping around Gung-Choux Village where we'd been staying with Uncle Crazy Wolf while we got things finalised over moving back to Phoenix Rise.

'Handold's place it is, Shy,' I said, climbing into the saddle and giving Grandma a hand up to take a seat behind me. Then we set off at a lope out of town. Shy knew to stay on the ground as Yenene hated flying.

We travelled in silence for much of

the way, which suited me fine. I was just enjoying being back on the eastern arm and took in the scenery like it was the first time I'd seen it. We rode to our neighbour-to-be's ranch to check on our steers then finally back to Gung-Choux Village just as the moon started to rise from behind the far hills.

No sooner had we ridden into the village than I became aware of a commotion at the foot of the great tribal totem pole. A few elf braves

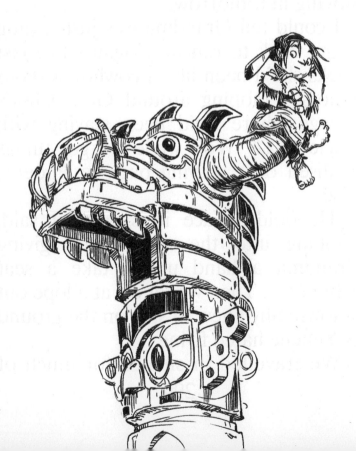

were in heated discussion, pointing and staring up at the top of the totem, and I was pretty sure I spotted Uncle Crazy Wolf among them.

Riding closer and dismounting, I saw the reason for the commotion. A young elf child had climbed the totem and now clung to one of the thunder-dragon's wings. He was crying. A group of female elves were calling up to him.

My uncle saw me approach and called, 'Will, you arrive at a crisis. A young adventurer, not unlike you when you were his age, has got himself stuck up there.'

I thought about flying Moonshine up to the top of the totem but it was a bit risky; the wind or one of Shy's wings could easily hit the child, knocking him off.

'I'll climb up and get him.'

'Will . . .' Grandma warned.

One of the female elves, her eyes full of tears, turned to me. 'Hail, Roaring Dragon, but it will not work. The pole is too unstable. I have already tried to climb, and the wobble of the pole almost shook my young one to his death. Bad storms have weakened its foundation.'

Hearing my elf-brave name filled me with a rush of pride. I took out a clean handkerchief and handed it to her. 'I think a little magic may be the only way to get your boy down safely.'

I took out some dried leaves and handed some to Crazy Wolf too.

'How about we conjure a wind ball then coax him to jump off?'

Crazy Wolf crushed some magic leaves into flakes between the palms of his hands. As he did so, he muttered some words in the elf tongue.

'Wumura Woha Anawa!'

I copied him, focusing my mind on the magic, as a ball of dark, cloud-like steam began to form above the palms of my hands, spinning furiously, whistling like a storm. The little boy looked down and started to cry even louder, clinging on tighter. My uncle's wind ball grew bigger like mine. Then both wind balls merged together to make one vast swirling ball of magic.

'Jump!' I cried up to the little boy. 'The wind ball will break your fall, you'll be fine.'

But the little boy just shook his head and kept on crying. Suddenly, I had an idea.

'I think he's gonna need a bit of non-magical persuasion,' I said, turning to the female elf. 'You said the pole was wobbly, can you give it a shake?'

She smiled nervously and nodded, then grabbed the bottom of the pole, pushing hard. The totem moved slightly then began to wobble back and forth. Soon the top jerked just enough to cause the elf kid to lose his grip. He screamed, and the gathered elves gasped as he plummeted towards the ground, but the wind ball had now stretched to become a stormy mass between my uncle and me. In a lightning-quick move, we caught the child in the middle of the swirling air.

'Well done, Roaring Dragon.' Crazy Wolf grinned. 'Good to have you back in the village.'

Yenene said nothing, but patted me on the arm and then walked with us back to my uncle's tepee.

Crazy Wolf soon had a fire roaring outside his tepee, over which he cooked us some supper: smoked gutfish and flatbread, washed down with a mug of hot coffee.

When we'd eaten we sat around and talked about the day.

Yenene handed me a couple of old leather-bound books. 'I got a confession to make,' she said. 'I hid these on ya long time ago.'

'My magic books.' A grin spread over my face; I thought about all the time I'd spent searching for them. 'But how come they didn't get burnt in the fire?'

'Hid them in a barrel behind the outhouse, so luckily they escaped the flames. I asked Tyrone to look them out for me.'

Then Yenene did something that took me even more by surprise. Dipping her finger into one of Crazy Wolf's face-paint pallets that lay near the fire, she smeared two bold red and yellow stripes onto my cheeks— the marks of an elf brave. When she'd finished she said, 'Ain't really had a chance to say sorry, Will, for being so hard on you about learning elf magic.'

I was doubly taken aback. Firstly that Grandma would put elf paint on my face but even more that she'd apologised. Yenene weren't the apologetic sort. 'That's OK, Grandma. You had a pretty good reason for acting the way you did.'

'That don't make it OK. I gave you a lot of grief at times—don't know how you put up with me, but I'm sorry. Heck, you're old enough to figure out what you wanna do, and if it's to be an elf mage then that's fine with me.'

'Thanks, Grandma, but that's just it . . . I'm not so sure I want to be a mage anymore.'

Uncle Crazy Wolf gasped.

Yenene stared at me, looking just as taken aback. 'You ain't?'

'No. To be honest, I've been thinking about joining the sky cavalry. The High Sheriff sent me a letter inviting me to the next recruitment session. Be working with Jez too.'

'The sky cavalry. But you . . .' she stopped.

'What?'

'Gotta learn to bite my tongue. Like
305

I say, you're old enough to figure out what you wanna do and if it's the sky cavalry then that's fine with me too. Can't say I won't worry 'bout you none, though.'

'Thanks. Uncle, you OK with that?'

He nodded. 'You must find your own way in this life, young Will. You would make a fine medicine mage, of this I have no doubt—but I have also no doubt that you would make a fine soldier. It is you who must choose the path.'

'It's just that I've been thinking. Being a mage you're really only serving the elf folk, whereas being in the sky cavalry you get to serve the whole o' the West Rock. And being a mix o' things, like I am, that suits me real well.'

Yenene sipped her coffee. 'Never thought of it like that before.'

'I'm still thinking about it, and if I do decide to join up it won't be this season. Wouldn't be fair on you, Grandma, what with you needing help settling into the new ranch, bringing over the cattle and

307

horses. And I'd still like to continue my studies in elf magic even if I do join the sky cavalry.'

'Well, whatever you decide is fine with me.'

Lifting a mirror, I checked out my cheeks. 'Nice job, Grandma, but where'd you learn how to put on elf paint?'

'A long time ago.' She smiled. 'I used to put Little Phoenix's on for her every morning, and there are some things that you never forget.'

The full moon bathed the village in pale ghostly light. The fearsome horned head of the thunder dragon at the top of the totem pole looked even more ferocious in the moonlight, its dagger-sharp teeth protruding up past its flared nostrils.

I yawned. 'Well, I think I'll turn in. Gonna be a big day tomorrow what with the move an' all.'

We said our good nights, then for the last time I rolled out my little fur-covered sleeping mat and lay on the floor of Uncle Crazy Wolf's tepee, staring up at the stars through the chimney hole. I was too tired to think of anything much except that it felt good to be back living on the eastern arm and that this time tomorrow night I'd be back in my old room in Phoenix Rise, in a proper bed with a comfy mattress. Tomorrow night I'd be home.

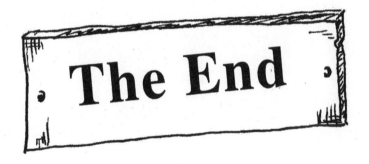